Critical acclaim for

'Danks is the queen of techno-crime... apocalyptic view of contemporary London (especially the East End): savage, gutted, greedy, abandoned to the barbarians. Hugely impressive'
Philip Oakes, *Literary Review*

'Danks is now firmly placed as one of Britain's few female noir writers – and probably the only computer noir crime writer'
The Times One Hundred Masters of Crime

'Danks brings all her writing skills to create a dark tale of voyeurism and betrayal, murder and attempted murder, as the characters dance a joyless saraband of sex without love and life without meaning'
Mark Timlin, *Independent on Sunday*

'. . . guns, fish hooks and rampant desire. Hot stuff and so typically un-British' *Time Out*

'The superlative Denise Danks . . . edgy and disturbing' *The Times*

'In her narrator Georgina – sexy, amoral and all too often hungover – [Denise Danks] has produced a figure who would undoubtedly get three stars in a Michelin guide to crime novel heroines' *Evening Standard*

'Georgina Powers is one of the few detectives who has really got to grips with technology. She is a wonderfully flawed heroine. This is Danks on top form' Maggie Pringle, *Express*

Denise Danks has been described by *The Times* as one of the six best crime writers in the UK. A journalist and a screenwriter, she is also the author of the Georgina Powers series of computer crime novels, the latest of which, *Phreak*, is also available as an Orion paperback. she is married with two children and lives in London.

By Denise Danks

The Pizza House Crash
Better Off Dead
Frame Grabber
Wink a Hopeful Eye
Phreak
Torso
Baby Love

BETTER OFF DEAD

Denise Danks

ORION

An Orion paperback

First published in Great Britain in 1991
by Macdonald & Co (Publishers) Ltd
This paperback edition published in 1992
by Futura

Reissued 2001
by Orion Books Ltd,
Orion House, 5 Upper St Martin's Lane,
London WC2H 9EA

A CIP catalogue record for this book is available
from the British Library.

ISBN 0 75284 379 6

Printed and bound in Great Britain by
Clays Ltd, St Ives plc

To my parents

Acknowledgements

My thanks to: Mark Turner of the Digital Equipment Company Limited for his advice, JFPR, *Music Week*, Jean McCann, child minder extraordinaire, and my old pal, Peter White, who thinks he deserves an acknowledgement for something.

Prologue

They say you always remember where you were when you heard the news that Johnny Waits was dead. He was the megastar of megastars, a supernova, even. So talented that some people believed he wasn't human at all, but a god come to earth with a golden guitar and lightning hands to wring the hearts of mankind and make more money than a poor boy from Huddersfield, which is what he was, could ever imagine was possible.

Of course he was human, and mortal, and at thirty-five years of age, he blew his addled, divine, brains out from the inside with an overdose of heroin. They say it's a hell of a way to go.

'That's another Waits record . . . fourth one in a row. Something must be up. When they die or something, the DJs dig out all their old classics, don't they? . . . He must have died or something,' said the girl in the white overall as she peered over my legs. She spread the hot sticky wax in long caramel-coloured strips on my pale shins like a chef spooning orange sauce on poultry. The radio was playing 'Cover me (I want your love)' – a Waits classic. Everything by Waits was a 'classic'.

She was right. Four in a row meant something serious had happened, presumably to Waits. I winced as she repeatedly pressed the cotton strips on the solidifying wax and tugged back sharply, ripping away the strip and leaving my tingling skin smooth and hairless as a plucked chicken underneath. The DJ began his slow patter . . . 'For everyone out there

1

who knew how great he was, four great classics from the one and only Johnny Waits, who, sadly, died last night . . . ' The smug, self-satisfied ads quickly followed: for the dandruff shampoo . . . la, la; la . . . for the toilet paper . . . shoo be doo . . . for the courier service . . . bee bop bee bop . . .

I watched a rash of red spots spread across my legs like chicken-pox. That's what you get after a glittering career at the zenith of rock stardom: three jingles for an epitaph.

'Sad, innit?' remarked my lightly-tanned torturer, scraping back a loose strand of her honey-coloured hair. 'Bikini line?'

I bit my lip and nodded, instantly regretting the decision as she spread the wax to the fringes of my pubic hair. It was too late; she was pressing a hand on my soft thigh to rip back with the other.

'All right?' she said, standing back a little to check that I was evenly skinned both sides.

'That'll do,' I said.

Smiling, she oiled her hands and smoothed them gently but firmly up and down my warm inflamed skin.

That was the day that Johnny Waits, the colossus of rock and roll, died. My friend Carla had invited me to her party and in a few hours my legs would look smooth, the spots would have gone and no one would suspect that my 15-denier sheen was anything but natural.

November 22nd. Yes, a tragic day, the DJ pointed out, excited by the coincidence. Twenty-five years ago to the day that someone had killed Kennedy from the window of the sixth floor of the Texas School-Book Depository in Dallas. They say it's going to be a $3.5 million visitors' centre and bookshop for the tourists to visit now. For four dollars, you'll be able to visit the sixth floor, look out of the south-east corner window and see Dealey Plaza along Elm Street. It'll be the high spot of an Assassination Weekend in Dallas. It was unfortunate that Waits's death wasn't so scenic.

November 22nd. A black day, a day for killing heroes, selling dead presidents, and rock 'n roll suicides.

Chapter 1

People were dancing in a small, dark, empty bedroom, and there was a strong smell of premium grade cannabis in the air. It was Carla's goodbye party. She was leaving low-rent Hackney for a five-bedroomed Georgian house in Islington – real Islington, not just Stoke Newington with Roman blinds. That's real money; what three number ones and a best-selling album bought you for starters.

'You've heard, I suppose?' I said as I came through the door and she kissed me on both cheeks.

Carla shrugged. 'Yeah. Sad, isn't it?' Then she tugged at my hand and led me nonchalantly through to the crowded room.

'I thought you'd be upset.'

'I am . . . but I met him, you know. Strange guy. Brilliant, of course, in his time, but really odd, bit of a junkie and into all this West Coast, new wave, crystal-rubbing stuff . . . thought we should blend auras, can you believe it? I told him my aura works alone, mate! Strange guy, but aren't they all?'

'Pop artists or men in general?'

'Pop artists and men in general. You drinking?'

'As I live and breathe.'

She grinned, and handed me a large plastic cup of gin and tonic. 'Cheers, then . . . ' She knocked her cup of Scotch against mine and looked around. The party crowd was pressing in, to be nearer to her. It was always like this now, even with friends. She was famous, and everyone she knew

3

to say good morning to was her friend. Carla could be as crass and as outrageous as she liked, and she could be both, but they would talk about it only in the context of her talent and innate star quality. Everything was forgivable, tolerated, so long as she remained a star and they could remain tied to her by a glutinous thread of familiarity. Just knowing somebody famous counted for something.

Carla turned her back on them and leaned nearer to me, looking up at me with those dark chocolate-coloured eyes. 'Seriously, any men?'

'I've given them up. My judgment is consistently poor on the subject.'

'Yeah, well, never mind, they're just a bloody waste of time.' Carla's head jerked sharply forward as someone pulled her backwards, spilling her drink. Her eyes opened wide and her eyebrows lifted as she lost her balance and fell back into the party crowd. She threw her arms out as if she was falling, confident that someone would catch her, laughing and crying out for help.

I waved to her as she danced. The music got louder. I looked around at the bobbing heads. I wanted to have fun, but I didn't feel as up now as I had when I arrived. Bloody waste of time. Why did it take so long to put the past behind you? Every time it was out of sight, a word, a place, a song would bring it all back and the next person you met got the wash of it all as your memories steamed by. I got myself another drink, and then another, until it was three o'clock and Carla decided we should leave. I was drunk, but she seemed sober.

'I don't have to stay here now,' she said, slipping her arm through mine and hustling me to the door. 'Come on. Come on! Let's go to my place. We'll sleep there. Come on. I'm inviting you to breakfast.'

Breakfast with Carla Blue, every Smiley kid's dream.

I liked her house. The large, empty, front room had high handsome ceilings and smooth, shiny, wooden floors. The sort of place you saw in magazine lifestyle features. There would be a smart couple pictured giving an elegant dinner party to tell their friends how much they had bought the place for, what they did to it, and what they could sell it for now. The place would have been run-down and neglected, but its features would have been intact. He would be an architect and she would illustrate children's books or work in fabrics. Of course, they had done most of the work themselves.

'This is a great place,' I said, dropping toast-crumbs on the floor.

Carla handed me a mug of coffee. 'Move in, if you like. I've got five bedrooms . . . and it's really too big for little old me.' She walked to the window, peered out and then turned back to look at me. The hazy light of morning began to edge across her face. 'Seriously, think about it . . . I need someone normal around. Well, not too normal,' she said.

'Thanks,' I said, walking over to the other window.

'You know what I mean.'

'Sure,' I replied, burning the roof of my mouth as I tried to swallow my drink. My breath and the steam from the coffee fogged up the glass. I wiped my hand down the window.

The house was quite close to the street, separated from the pavement by tall spiked railings. Across the road was a small tree-edged square with big heaps of brown leaves swept up in the corners. Thinking about it, it wasn't a bad idea. This spacious old-world splendour had to be better than my concrete box in the sky in Bow. It was nearer to town. People cycled to work from here. I'd have nowhere to cycle to, though.

Carla kept talking. 'Look, the house is paid for. I'll put in two telephone lines so you can work without my lot hassling you . . . What do you reckon?'

It sounded perfect, but I didn't answer. We both peered out of the high sash windows. My forehead was pressed against the cool glass. I wanted to close my eyes and sleep right there. Why was she making me think now? I couldn't concentrate on this house, I thought about the lives I'd shared in other houses. I thought about my ex-husband Eddie Powers and his mistress. I thought about my ex-friend Warren Graham, tidying up after me – and he hadn't even moved in. Tidying up. Sobering me up. Double-crossing me. Loving me.

'Hello? Anybody there?' I turned away from the window, and Carla had topped up my coffee-cup. 'What do you reckon?'

'What?'

'About moving in here. Haven't you been listening?'

I was surprised to see her standing there close to me. She looked so real and solid, and I was drifting. 'Sorry . . . Thanks. But no thanks.'

'Why not?'

Why not? It was a simple question, but the answer would be too complicated. I couldn't really explain now. I didn't want to explain. 'I'm all right where I am,' I said, resting my cheek against the windowpane.

She didn't push it. She just sighed and walked over to her window-ledge, lifting herself on to it and looking outside. The morning sun was streaming in, picking out the dust in shafts of light. Our shadows stretched out across the sand-coloured floor. 'Nice here, though, isn't it?' She lifted her knees up and hugged them to her chest. 'Oooh, I do so like being rich!'

Yes. It was better than being poor. But she had never been poor, and neither had I. Not really. We'd been a bit short, that's all. We'd never really starved, never begged or slept in a cardboard box under a damp bridge. But what was rich? Purchasing power? Buying things? Like houses and cars and clothes? Carla had been short only because she wouldn't get a decent job. She'd always had a good time. No. It wasn't being rich she liked so much. She loved the glamour. She really liked that. She should have said that.

'Are you all right for money?' she said. 'Is that it? I told you the house is paid for. I wouldn't charge you rent.'

I was all right for money. I was. Not many people had gained from the great stock market crash of 1987, but I had, without even trying. I hadn't bought a house or a car. I hadn't spent it on anything except living. My savings had come in very handy for a year since I quit my job at *Technology Week*, the top computer industry newspaper in the business. I'd rowed with my boss over a story, and I hadn't worked since. Not because of him, but because of me. I had no appetite for reporting any more, and I hadn't even tried to think of other things to do. Instead, I'd left town for sunny Spain and got back to London just as the pink blossoms had started to show on the grimy trees. The first person I'd called was Carla.

'I can't believe that Sweat Box gig was just eight months ago,' I said, changing the subject.

'It seems like ages, doesn't it?'

'You know, if I hadn't been on the liggers' list I wouldn't have got in. The black guy on the door, the one with the shrapnel skin and the jewel stuck in his nose, looked at me as if I had something on the underside of my shoe.'

'Yeah, that's Darren. He thinks a lot of himself. He nearly didn't let me in, and I was the act.'

I took my head off the window and turned to look at her. She was gazing out of the window, and smiling. That was the night that Ghea Records signed her up, and my pal Charlotte Ball became Carla Blue forever. 'I was late. Your set had already started. I couldn't believe how much you'd changed, jigging about in a black bra, black cycling shorts and all that red chiffon sticking out like a huge flaming tutu. You looked a prat.'

She turned to me, still smiling. 'Well, it worked, didn't it? What about the guys' Surf Nazi look? You know, I don't think either of them can even swim.'

We both laughed.

'Well, everyone was into it. Walk down any street in the city and you'd think you were at Huntingdon Beach, California,' I said.

'Remember those amazing air-cooled Reeboks of Mick's?'

'And those mean, black, wraparound Raybans? Dead cool.'

'You know why they called themselves Big, don't you?' she said. I shook my head, imagining some puerile phallic joke that the boys had shared. 'It was Keith's idea. It was so when they went on tour, they could say they were Big in Manchester – or Tokyo, come to that. He thought it was funny. In the end they weren't big anywhere.'

'No.' I felt shamefaced for her.

'Mick was the serious one. So damned serious, with his little, beige, po-faced computer, standing over his keyboard like he was stuffing bread dough into the thing with his hands.'

'Well, you could hardly accuse Keith of taking it seriously. He looked like the Red Baron on a Virgin flight to Miami.'

'Didn't he just! Those Day-Glo surf shorts and dark, satanic, industrial glasses with the leather flaps at the side. Wasn't he a killer? He couldn't play that sax to save his life, either. He liked it, though, said it turned the girls on. Can you believe that? "Look at this, baby, now imagine my dick" sort of thing. We carried him. I'm telling you. But don't be fooled, he was serious all right.'

'If you say so; but he wasn't that bad. I thought he lightened up the set considerably,' I said.

'Oh, come on! Forget the sax. What about the guitar work? That killed me, strumming away like he was fluffing up a rug.'

'Maybe you're right. But it did sound pretty good, all in all, and he made sure you got goosed frequently enough.'

Carla stopped laughing. 'Yeah, well. He thought he could use me, but he was the one that got goosed in the end, didn't he? The pair of them, nicely goosed,' she said and jumped off the windowsill. Then she walked out of the room. 'More coffee?' she called over her shoulder.

I didn't answer. All of a sudden I felt guilty because Mick, whose real name was George, and Keith, whose real name was David, were both our friends. They were fun, and without them no one would ever have noticed Carla Blue. She'd needed them then.

The crowd had been stacked into the place that night and it was jungle hot. Condensation poured off the black brick walls like sweat off a weightlifter's back and amoebic blobs of coloured light ebbed and flowed on the faces of the tightly packed dancers. They were all smiling, all dancing, all sweating, all young. The strobes framed their arms and their heads in the rapid beat, and the pounding bass was loud. It vibrated up through the black and white checked floor and bounced off the low subterranean ceiling. You could feel it rippling down your arm and frothing the beer in the can in your hand. But these kids were wild-eyed from drinking orange juice, their damp ringlets caught back by 'Don't tell me, it's Springsteen' bandanas. They jumped up and down in their huge, baggy, brightly coloured T-shirts and loud shorts. Their feet pumped up and down in hi-tech box-fresh running shoes. It was a workout, a reach and reach and stretch and stretch workout. Their bodies were twisting so fast that sometimes it looked as if they had their legs on back to front. I'd felt out of it, tame and dissipated at one and the same time with my alcohol, my little black dress and big black Doctor Martens.

Come to think of it, the only two other people in the place who looked as tame were the tall blond Christian Dexter and his drinking partner, John St John, a stocky, sandy-haired army type, sweating in an expensive, baggy, light-coloured suit. At least Dexter looked cool with his little ponytail, faded Levi 501s and alligator motif polo shirt. But they had nothing to worry about. They had power. Dexter was Ghea Records' A&R man and St John was Carla's manager, and we all three sheltered by the bar and watched the show. St John nudged Dexter. Carla was ramping up for her big scream at the start of her Waits-sampled club hit 'Why

9

doncha cover me (I want your love)?' Her pelvis seemed to be screwing her feet to the floor. I looked over at the Ghea man, but he didn't move a muscle. He just kept his eyes right ahead. St John looked as if he were about to catch fire and then the crowd went crazy. Keith was goosing Carla with a vengeance. Mick was stuffing the keyboard. It was so wild, they did the extended remix version twice.

Yes, that was the night Christian Dexter went backstage and told them that Ghea Records wanted Carla, and John St John told Mick and Keith they were out. The boys were understandably upset.

'Fuck right off!' Mick said, peeling the top off a can of beer so that everyone in the room but him caught the pleasantly cool spray.

Carla, Keith and I were cramped together on a table by a sticker-covered mirror, and Mick, Dexter and St John were standing up. There wasn't enough room to swing a right or a left, so the language got progressively worse.

Carla didn't say very much, and Mick seemed much more upset than Keith. Keith sat back with the top of his sweaty head leaning against the mirror, staring at the ceiling while Mick and St John did the shouting. Dexter hung back as well, while St John, compact, muscular and immovable as a pit bull terrier, held firm for his 10, 15, 20 per cent of something.

It took about a quarter of an hour of abusive exchanges for the deep-voiced Dexter to raise his voice and quieten the room. 'Look, forget it, boys, OK? It's over. Carla, listen to me. You've got a great future. You're going to be a star. You've got it. Just you, not them.' He was looking right at her, holding her gaze, speaking slowly, meaningfully, as if he was saying he loved her. It was a fine interpretation of Svengali's script and Carla soaked it in. Mick crunched his beer-can in his hand and groaned in disgust, but no one else did a thing. This is the stuff that rock dreams are made of, in places that smelled of fresh sweat and hot feet and measured six by four, like the dressing-room of the legendary Sweat Box.

That was it. Carla signed and Big didn't. But Big made something out of it. Well, the first hit, at least. Ghea Records had some big names on its books and Johnny Waits was one of the biggest. Carla and Big had sampled heavily from his song 'Cover me, I want your love', for 'Why doncha cover me .. ?' – their club hit – and after Carla signed, no one hassled them with petty accusations of plagiarism. Instead, Ghea remixed and marketed their song with a video featuring old tape of Johnny Waits's performance and Carla's pelvis. It went to number one. The lean, wild man Waits and my anarchic friend Carla were a seductive combination that spelled S-E-X, and in marketing terms that spells a free ride in big easy-to-read letters.

She came back with a couple more mugs of steaming coffee in one hand and another plate of hot toast and ginger marmalade in the other. 'Sorry, this lot is instant,' she said.

'I'll take it,' I said. My head was beginning to ache. I noticed this more often nowadays. How the hangovers began before the party was over.

She sat down near me, on the floor this time, and set the plate down in front of her. 'You know, Waits sold more albums this Christmas than he'd done in the past five years?' she said.

'Oh, that's a comfort, isn't it,' I replied, motioning to her to pass the toast.

'Well, he was going nowhere before "Why doncha" came along. That boosted his album sales, for a start. There was even talk of a new album.'

'So what'll happen now?' I said.

'I think they'll get together an album of out-takes and a few of the tracks he was working on when he died. God, he couldn't have done better had he done a charity gig. I mean, dying like that.'

'Yes. I suppose in your business they call it the ultimate career move,' I said, and Carla winced at my tone.

'Oh, come on! It's not my bloody fault, is it? It just so

happens to be true. Can't I talk to you?'

I made a face at her and, in retaliation, she pushed the plate of toast out of my reach. She was right. The morning papers had probably begun to canonise him already, and Ghea had already started pressing extra copies of his albums to meet the excess demand. I looked out of the window again. The light was very bright now and hurt my eyes. I wanted to close them and go to sleep.

Carla stood up and put her hand on my shoulder. 'Come on. There's only one bed, but we'll manage, won't we?'

I think we did. Under her pillow, Carla kept a vibrator against which I managed to knock my head. As I held the trophy up to her face like an Olympic torch, she explained that it was a gift from St John. He said it was the only way to survive on tour nowadays, things being what they were. I said it was a hell of a way to make a point about safe sex, and the last thing I remember was Carla giggling and telling me I had nice little tits.

Chapter 2

Six months later, she was at my place poking around my desk. I didn't care, I hadn't used it in a long time.

'What you doing nowadays?'

'Nothing much.'

'You're not working for *Technology Week* or anyone, then?'

'Nope.'

'Why?'

'Disagreement on standards.'

Carla made a face at my moral tone, so I explained a little. 'I did a story on an international financial scandal and got stuffed. It involved my ex, Eddie, and a good friend, you know, Warren Graham. He was a computer buff, let's say. This used to be his flat. That's basically it. OK?'

'So why don't you write about computers any more?'

'I do sometimes . . . I'm on sabbatical.'

'Oh, I get it. You can't think what to do, but you've got enough money to sit around while you think about it.'

'In one. What time is it?'

'Eight o'clock. You going to eat?' she said, walking into my small kitchen with its wondrous view of the uniform stacked balconies of the twin tower blocks looming to neck-breaking heights above.

'What've we got?'

'Nothing.'

'Dial a pizza or do you want to eat out?'

'Dial a pizza, but it might not come here.'

My flat was on the sixth floor of a housing association block in Bow. If the lift worked, we might get the pizza, but there was no guarantee that the delivery moped would still be there when the guy got down again. Pizza delivery personnel also got mugged nowadays, for the pizzas and their money. These things had to be taken into consideration. I didn't have to explain the details to Carla who, before her rebirth as a rich rock star, had lived in a hard-to-let in the London Borough of Hackney. That place had made my tenement look like Hearst Castle.

The pizzas did arrive, and the Chinese delivery-man handed over the boxes like they were contraband, took the money and ran.

'I've got to take a year out,' Carla muttered, as I sliced the pizzas in two and served the halves on to our plates.

'What do you mean?'

'Tax. My accountant says I have to take a year abroad.'

'Well! That means you've cracked it, Carla. You're going to be a tax exile . . . five monster hits in a year, the album, the tour . . . Now do I get to drive your car? Beep, beep. Beep, beep. Yeah?'

'It's not funny. The last one wasn't that monster, anyway. It went up, and it came down. The single only went to number two and didn't stay. I owe £200,000 and God knows how much National Insurance – people forget about that – which means the next £200,000 I earn goes to pay them off, the Inland Revenue. But I get taxed on that as well, so all I'll be doing is working for the taxman from now on unless I get out. Charlie Wingrove, my accountant, says if I leave for a year, I can come back for sixty days the following year. If I do that, the money from the new album, which I have to record abroad and get out before Christmas, will go towards paying the tax I owe, but that at least will be tax free.'

'That's good,' I said, but she hardly noticed.

'Do you know they have an Entertainers Unit of the Inland Revenue in some bleeding place in Watford, who read the *Financial Times* and *New Musical Express* – they read every bloody music paper. They spend their mean little days collecting newspaper cuttings, my cuttings, and dodging in and out of data banks to keep track of what I'm doing! The bastards . . . Shit . . . I don't want to go, Georgie. They're forcing me.'

I shook my head. Dear, oh dear. 'Look. Top-rate tax is only 40 per cent now – why not pay it?'

She gave me a look which urged me to think of alternatives.

'Or get into one of those artificial loss-making scams. Allowable tax losses, that's what they are officially. Even Cliff 'God on my Side' Richards has done it. Investing in pine trees is out now, even if I'd let you do it. But there's still freight-container leasing. I read it somewhere. Or you can tuck away £40,000 into a business expansion scheme.'

Carla didn't appear to be listening.

'OK. What about a pension plan? Yes, what about that? Nice and simple.'

She picked up a slice of pizza, bit it and talked through the strings of elasticated cheese. 'Gimme a break. Where'd you get all that stuff? Have you got a fucking pension? No. Come on, I can't think about me at sixty. I'm a pop star, don't you know? Probably won't even reach thirty, never mind sixty!'

'That gives you three years. What are you planning?'

She just waved her hand at me like I was a bothersome fly and looked around for the wine. This time, she stopped eating to explain. 'My accountant says I've got to incorporate myself and then piss off and earn like stink. After sixty days I can come back for ten days, and after six months, thirty days, etcetera etcetera. I have to be abroad for twelve months minus no more than a sixth, but it works on a sliding scale. That's how it works. I don't have to go very far, just to Eire, and if I stay on, I could qualify for tax exemption if I can prove myself of artistic merit to some committee there.'

I poured two very large glasses of cold Chianti. She really

15

had a grasp of the situation, but I tried to make her look on the positive side. 'Don't they have some sort of club for ex-pat tax exile rock stars in Dublin?'

'The White Elephants Club or something. 'Bout right, 'cos they've all been forgotten. If you go ex-pat, that's what happens. There're no women. Full of dorks and their chicks or dorks and their dorks. Great.'

We chewed silently through the pizzas and finished the wine. It was wonderful, dry as old parchment, and I got up to search for another bottle.

'I don't want to go,' she said, brushing crumbs from her face. 'I just don't want to.'

'Charlie, you can go somewhere nice. The Caribbean. If not, Dublin's a great crack, so they say.'

'You've been there?'

'Once. Once on a press trip.'

'Great.'

I wasn't being much help, and she was beginning to look very agitated. 'Look, stuff that, I *like* London. I *need* to work in the UK. It's my biggest market. It's my home market. John St John says I should tour the US, then record an album, maybe in Eire, then take a break somewhere and then do some more recording. For once, I don't agree. Being away could kill me, my fans'll forget about me, and I don't know these new guys in the band that well to do a big tour. I don't feel . . . confident about this.' Large wet tear drops dripped from her big brown eyes while her perfect little nose turned pink and snivelly. She was really crying.

I dug for a tissue in my jeans pocket. This was terrible. 'Surely the US tour is what you need, Charlie? You've had a couple of hits there now, surely you need to perform over there to make it really big. You can take advantage of this year out,' I said, trying to comfort her by taking her damp hand.

She put her other hand over mine. 'I want you to come.'

'But I can't. I can't just drop everything.'

'Drop what?'

16

I took back my hand, and staring at her over the rim, put the glass to my lips. She was right. Drop what? I was alone, divorced, rarely sober, bored with writing and not writing, bored wasting time, bored with living; but I didn't want to be reminded of it.

'Cover the tour. Do the story of the tour. I'll give you complete authorisation. You could get a great advance for that. Come with me. Please!'

It was tempting. After all, what had I to lose? She was right, it could be a nice little earner for me. On the other hand, I liked being independent, an independent friend. But, still, it would be an absolute gas, an unrepeatable wild experience. It was a great idea. I made up my mind quickly. I did want to do it, but I wanted to tease her, too. 'Well, I dunno . . . ' I said, deadly serious, eyebrows up, eyes down.

But Carla misread me. She didn't see the joke and she mistimed her reply. It wasn't like her at all, but she was too anxious to be cautious. 'You've got to come. I need you,' she said, pulling my head up by the chin. 'Georgina, I can't not see you for months on end. I love you. Don't you know that? I love you.'

That was it. Three little words, and the whole world as you know it shifts on its axis. I didn't really know what to say, so I laughed a little instead and pushed her hand away. 'You cannot be serious!' I was still laughing, a little nervous now.

Carla got up, pressed her fists straight down on the kitchen table. I thought she was going to shout, but she spoke to me as carefully as she would to a child. 'Of course I'm serious, you fool! What do you think I am? Are you totally blind? And what about you, are you sure about yourself? Why is it all so funny?'

The questions streamed into my head but I really couldn't answer her. My mouth was dry with shock. I stared at her instead, my hands clasping my half-empty glass. Carla famous, Carla, blonde and seductive, the Blue Siren, the Generation Girl, the wet dream of a dozen Fleet Street subs,

17

the cover girl guaranteed to sell millions upon millions of glossy magazines with one wicked, but wholesome, smile.

I knew who she really was. She was Charlotte Ball, school chum, the one who was too small to borrow my clothes and never give them back, the one who always played an angel in the Nativity play while I played a shepherd, and drank a bottle of Quink ink in thirty seconds for my week's tuckshop money. She was a friend, a pal. A drinking, dancing, partying, eating, talking, teasing, crying, laughing bosom pal. I knew that smile. I knew *her*. This wasn't what I knew. What had I done to make her think things had changed? We'd spent a lot of time together, We were friends, real friends, that's all. My, but she'd grown some. I looked up, and she was glaring down at me, those dark brown eyes, wet and shiny, her body tense, her mouth screwed up with anger and distress.

'I don't understand . . . '

Carla rolled her eyes in frustration, sat down and leaned on the table, putting her hands to her temples. 'I love you. You know what that means, don't you? Love isn't just a sweet thing that happens between boys and girls, you know. For God's sake! I can't believe you didn't know. I thought you understood.'

'Believe it,' I replied stiffly, wiping my fingers on some kitchen roll. We sat there in silence. I couldn't think of a single question to ask her that wouldn't make me sound like a cross between counsellor and voyeur, a single thing to say that wouldn't sound insincere. I just couldn't look her in the eye. It was embarrassing. She made me feel like a prude. I could feel her exasperation eating up the space between us.

Carla helped me out, a callous tone in her voice. 'I thought you'd given up on men.'

'That doesn't mean I've taken up with women. I'm just cutting out for a while. Men turn me on, that's my problem. Women don't, but I didn't think that was.'

'Oh, for God's sake. You'd spend forever contemplating your fluff-filled navel. What you really need is someone to do it for you. I could do it. I can read you like a book, I know what's eating you. George, I could turn you on.'

'Right on, sister.'

It was a verbal slap, and Carla's face tightened as if my hand had connected with her cheek. 'Oh, I get it! Right on, sister. Very good. Lesbianism means slogans, sisterhood, feminism, the struggle against sexual stereotypes and male dominance, dungarees, militant socialism, the loony Left, the campaign against nuclear disarmament, Greenham Common, green issues, save the whale, and maybe, right at the end of the list, porn movies . . . You know, Lesbian love, oh yes! What a turn-on. Passion, romance and sex between two women don't really come into it because lesbianism's fundamentally a political statement against a heterosexual society's conditioning of the sexes . . . well, fuck me, at least you won't catch anything.'

'Jee . . . sus, Carla.' I tried to drink more wine, but just ended up twiddling my glass around. I could feel my cheeks burning.

Carla began again. 'Do you love me?' Her voice was suddenly vulnerable and shy, her soft hand taking mine again.

I did the worst thing possible. I pulled my hand back and looked away. She sat still for a while, and then she leaned right over and kissed me hard, full on the mouth, leaving the intoxicating Italian aroma of expensive lipstick, oregano, and Chianti on my cold lips. For a moment I closed my eyes, and now that she was dead, I wished so much that I had kissed her back.

Her naked body had lain as cold and damp as the dog's nose snuffling towards it across the beach, head back, mouth full of the same silvery sand which speckled her eyes like sleep. Poor Carla: too happy to scream, too high to float, too numb to feel the water pouring into her mouth and the chill grip on her heart. Out of her head, swept far out into the dark, away from the party lights shining bright in the white villa, and away from the music and laughter dancing on the warm wind.

She'd been on her way home for Christmas, but Christian Dexter had invited her to his white villa which stood in wealthy isolation and tumbling red and lilac bougainvillaea above the tall Spanish cliffs. Below its wide semicircular terrace, the dark swimming-pool was low enough to be refreshed by the Atlantic rollers that swelled up against the rocks when the tide was high. There had been an all-night party, and some time in the early morning Carla had gone down to the pool for a swim.

I was home, safe and warm and slightly hungover, in bed when I heard about Carla. I'd listened to three of her records played in succession on the digital clock radio.

It had to be confirmed by the DJ. 'Yes, three songs in memory of the much-loved Carla Blue, probably the most promising young star of her generation, who, sadly, died in the early hours of this morning.'

It was a golden, bright, autumnal morning and the sun showed up the grimy dusty circles left by old raindrops on the windowpane as I lay, miserable, in bed, with the radio on. It was my first day back to work.

The first commission I had done in more than two years, and it was a PR job, not a real job, a favour for someone. Why had I taken so long to even get to that? Had I really given up? Two years of nothing, two wasted years, and whose fault was it? Sometimes I blamed the wasted time on my divorce, sometimes on the men I'd tried to love afterwards, sometimes on my old employers – but mainly I blamed myself for letting all that get to me. The disappointments had crushed me. My husband had been a disappointment, my lovers, my job and me, I had been a disappointment. I had thought I could stick a finger up at them and tough it out, but I couldn't, and now I wanted to get back in and work at something, do something, because there really wasn't anything much better, no green grass over the hill.

And now she was gone. We hadn't spoken in six months. She'd called once and I'd played her voice back on my answering machine. The tour was taking it out of her and she wanted me to meet her in Chicago. I'd called back, but I must have missed her, and the worst thing was, I was glad.

Now I stood in a sunny graphics studio in Surrey, staring at Carla's face on the sleeve of her new unreleased album, 'Seethru', big watery tears in my eyes. I could hardly bear to look at the red and black cover. Carla's white, fine-boned face turned to one side, head tilted back against the night-black background. Her heavy lids closed over those chocolate-coloured eyes, her sticky, plum-red lips parted, so you could see a glimpse of sugar-white teeth and a pink tongue. She wore what we had called the 'I ain't faking it' look for when we were. A ribbon of diaphanous red chiffon oozed like plasma from her short, golden hair, across her white neck, leaving her equally pale, half-exposed breasts blushing strawberry pink, pressed together into smooth, rounded, marshmallow curves by her pale arms. The newly available, almost edible Carla Blue, beautiful and shrink-wrapped, aroused, vulnerable, untouchable, lying next to the guitar-shaded, denim-clad crotch on the cover of 'The Unreleased Johnny Waits'. Two dead stars, the dream ticket, lying silently side by side.

'Ghea Records are very good customers,' said the tall grey-haired man who was looking over my shoulder. 'Seventy-five per cent of our work comes from music publishing – the single, album, cassette and compact disk covers, as well as posters for all the big record companies. We handle the printing here, too. The rest of our work comes from magazine houses – we handle a variety of magazines, including *Which Telephone* and *Puppetmaster* – the kids' comic.'

I nodded sagely, as if I took these worthy journals on subscription.

His bony finger pointed down over my shoulder shadowing Carla's image. 'Shame about the girl, isn't it?

Absolutely gorgeous. Success kills them, you know; they can't handle it. Too much of everything. Too much drink and drugs, I suppose, too much of the other . . . and God knows what else. We see a lot of this in the music business.'

God knows what else? Was there anything else? Drink, drugs, sex, rock and roll . . . that had to cover just about everything the latter half of the twentieth century had to offer by way of self-indulgence. What did he know about rock stars, about Carla? He probably listened to James Last on his in-car stereo. Humming along as he drove home along a green-banked dual carriageway to his modern brick three-bedroomed home. A house which I'd bet was embedded in two squares of green grass edged with wallflowers, tucked into a tarmacadam whorl of a cul-de-sac.

'Now that's what I call music,' he'd say to his blank-faced fifteen-year-old daughter, whose head rocked, safely wedged between a pair of miniature headphones.

I blinked and looked up. What was I doing here? This job wasn't that important. I didn't need the money, not yet. But I wasn't doing it for the money, though it was good. It was a restart for me. They were paying two hundred and fifty pounds a day for some undemanding, but competent, writing. It was nearly three times the daily rate that a computer newspaper, like *Technology Week*, paid. It wasn't journalism, but it was related, and it wasn't that hard. The story would have to put the client in a good light, that was what I was being paid for. The piece would be placed, with or without a by-line, in an appropriate magazine or newspaper so that the client got valuable publicity at considerably less cost than an ad, and the paper, squeezed on budgets, got some editorial free. I got an improved cash-flow and a gentle shove back to work. So everyone – but the reader – got a good deal, and he got the magazine free, anyway, so who was complaining?

The client had installed a one-million-pound computer-ised graphics system at this gentleman's print shop. It was a neat system that comprised a scanner, which electronically scanned, and then digitised, original artwork and transparencies so that they could be displayed on a computer screen. An artist could then manipulate the digitised images on screen to get the right tints, tones, shadows and graphics – something that would take hours if done manually. When he, OK or she, had finished, they pressed a button and the whole lot was output on to film ready for printing. What made the system special was its digital link with another office in Los Angeles. It meant that the team could start work in the morning in Surrey and a few hours later be ready to pass the record sleeves, with all their complex tints and graphics, to an imaging computer in California. The US team could then add the local credits, output the films and print their version over there, immediately.

'The digital link means the sleeve arrives the same day that it was produced and sent. There's an eight-hour time difference, you see. Depending on the size of the job, it can take ten minutes or up to four hours to send it. It's terrific for the record companies because they can get their product around the world so much faster. Instead of relying on couriers, who can take days or weeks and can be intercepted, you press a button, and . . . boomph! Up to the satellite and down. It's right there, on time, secure and fast. That's important for Ghea, for example, who are planning two simultaneous triple-format – CD, cassette and LP – releases, Johnny Waits and Carla Blue, worldwide next Friday, ready for the Christmas rush. Timing is so important . . . and what with Carla Blue dying, the demand is going to be *enormous*!'

She had been swept into the sea from a swimming-pool sculpted from rocks in a cliff-face, a year to the day that Johnny Waits had taken his last trip. November 22nd. The tabloids didn't miss the connection. She had belonged to everyone, they said. They used an old picture of him and the one from her 'Night Drive' album on a double-page spread. A GENERATION MOURNS, the large black headline wept and, yea, a whole generation went forth into the shops and bought her merchandise in great numbers. She couldn't have done better had she done a charity gig. Poor Carla, the career girl, had made the ultimate career move.

And there she was, permanently turned on in glossy four-colour. As I looked down, I struggled to keep my self-control while a raging shout built up from the bottom of my chest. I clenched my hands hard, let them go and the tension eased. He was right, of course, her album would accumulate extra sales like a meteor extending its tail across the arch of the sky. She had had the foresight to die just before Christmas and get the ball rolling. A grubby snowball, like Halley's Comet, dead impressive from a distance, but a big pile of universal shit when you got up close.

'Listen to this! C'mon, c'mon, leave that, listen to this . . . '

Carla was jumping up and down on the sofa with excitement. She pulled the earphones off her head and unplugged them, and the sound of a radio jingle filled the room. It was a phone-in, and Carla loved listening to phone-ins when she was in. She believed you learned a lot about people from phone-ins. You learn a lot about people who phone-in from phone-ins, I had remarked.

'After this, after this . . . someone's got lobsters!' she said.

'Surely you mean crabs?' I said, putting down my book.

'No, you silly cow. It's not that problem hour. It's the animal psychologist. People ring in because they want help with their animal's behaviour, but all the time you know it's their fault, they're the problem, because they're crazy. They can't treat their animals as animals, you see. They give their dogs chocdrops, French kisses and let them sleep in their beds. They put their budgie alone in a cage with sawdust at the bottom and wonder why it's so bored that it's picking its feet to bits. If the bird could masturbate, it would, just to pass the fucking time. You got to listen to some of these . . . Some woman from Dagenham's got a problem with her lobsters. She wants this guy to psychoanalyse her fucking lobsters.'

The jingle ended. 'Hi, Pat, this is Steve Webb speaking, welcome to the show. What do you want to ask our animal psychologist, Charles Fairweather?'

'Me lobsters ain't very well. I bought 'em for me tank. And one of 'em's shed its skin and died and the other one don't look very well, he keeps spinning around on 'is back. Can you tell me what's the matter wiv 'im?'

Carla's face was contorted with laughter. I thought she was about to asphyxiate. She was holding a cushion in her hand and thumping it.

'Well, you've got me there, Pat,' said the hapless Charles Fairweather. 'I don't know very much about marine animals. I mean . . . You are sure they are lobsters and not crayfish?'

'No. They're definitely lobsters. I bought 'em from the pet shop as lobsters.'

'Well, Pat, that is strange . . . They're obviously not very happy. And how do you keep your salt-water tank? Are you keeping it fairly . . . uh . . . well balanced and clean?' said Fairweather, eager to give Pat from Dagenham a fair go.

'No.'

'You're not?'

'No, it ain't salt water, I got a fresh-water tank.'

The broadcast gulp was Steve Webb stifling a laugh. 'Ah, well, in that case . . . they are suffering extreme demineralisation and will surely die. These are marine animals and cannot survive in fresh water. They need salt water, Pat, and your pet shop should have told you so. Good gracious! It's like taking a human being on Mars and expecting him to live. It is just not the right environment. Quite ridiculous!' Fairweather spoke gently at first, but his voice rose to a squeaky high pitch of admonishment before Steve Webb wrapped it up with a fun-loving chortle.

'No psychology to it, Pat. If you put things in the wrong environment they shed their skins, float on their backs, do funny things and die. You might as well have hit them over the head, put them in a pot and eaten them. Mmmm . . . lovely. Sorry, Pat. Now, who have we got on the line? Charlie . . . He's got a problem with his Rottweiler. It keeps eating things . . . '

I stared in wide-eyed horror at Carla, and she stared back at me. The shock lasted about thirty seconds before we fell back laughing, tears rolling down our aching cheeks. Poor Pat of Dagenham. She might as well have hit them over the head, put them in a pot and eaten them. Lobsters. All armoured up but vulnerable to water.

Mr Showbusiness had stopped talking, so I picked my notebook off the desk and rose to go.

'Have these,' he said, thrusting two copies of the cover pictures into my hands.

It was Carla's picture I looked at going home on the train. This picture was going to be reproduced a million times over to sell that many albums. She'd wanted me to see her like this. Now everyone was going to have chance to see her, in the erubescent pink. But it was a fake, a counterfeit. She was cold and dead, her mauve mouth gaping, her lips black, her damp yellow head lolling back, her flesh grey. There was no faking that. It was no little death, it was the Big One. She'd spun around on her back and died, like a lobster in a hostile fresh-water tank, a creature in the wrong environment, a victim of ignorance. It really wasn't funny.

Chapter 3

I went to Camden Lock on Sunday morning. I went on the pretext of looking for Christmas presents even though it was far too early for me. It got me out of my lonely flat with its telephone ringing and no news that I wanted to hear. But as soon as I saw the crowds, that pit-in-the-stomach feeling returned. It was an aching expectancy of finding something that you had lost, urging you forward to every likely face or corner and carrying you along with a somehow joyous pain of self-deception. She could be here, or there, it said, wouldn't that be great?

I took my jacket off and hung it over my shoulder as I walked past the bright, woollen knits and wooden toys on the stalls. It was another one of those unusually warm days before winter, when the trees shed the brown remnants of their dry leaves and seal themselves in before the onset of frost.

'Carla Blue. "Seefroo". Johnny Waits. Unreleased. £2.99 a tape. Wot an offer.'

The monotonous nasal voice was to my right, and I turned quickly to see a young man of medium height, with glossy, dark, shoulder-length hair and a golden earring, lift up a cassette, hold it in the palm of his hand and show it around to the curious passers-by. He had a cigarette cupped in the palm of his other hand, which he held furtively behind his back, while he scuffed his feet on the pavement. Blue and white smoke drifted from behind him in the light breeze.

He was a fly-pitcher, which meant he didn't pay for his

pitch like market stallholders were supposed to. He just dragged over his suitcase of goodies, opened it up between the other stalls on the pavement and began his business while keeping a wary eye open for the police or market officials. There was quite a crowd gathering around him, and it was not surprising. He had stacks of new cassettes lying in an open suitcase on the ground. When I pushed through to the front, I recognised some of the tape covers. The last time I had seen the artwork was in Surrey the day after Carla had died.

Ghea Records hadn't even released the albums, so how did this guy get them? Most pirate cassettes are copied from tapes bought in shops. The pirate sticks the legitimate tape in a duplicating machine and runs off a few thousand. But the cassettes, the CDs, the LPs, the videos of Carla Blue's "Seethru" and "The Unreleased Johnny Waits" weren't in the stores, and yet this guy was flogging cassette versions like hot samosas off his street stall. Carla Blue's "Seethru" and "The Unreleased Johnny Waits", the dream ticket.

'Awight, Tommy! Yo!' Someone called from across the street. 'On yer toes!'

Tommy's nicotine-stained fingers moved quickly, trying to cram cassettes and money back into his suitcase before whoever it was his mark had spotted came into view.

I rammed both hands into the case before he could get it shut and grabbed one of each cassette.

'Leave off, love! Wotcha doin'?'

'Got to have these,' I said. 'Here's six quid. Keep the change.'

With that he slammed the almost empty case shut and strolled nonchalantly across the street and into a pub. He was an East Ender, you could tell from the wide-boy walk, a kind of pigeon-toed heel-to-toe gait with shoulders pushed alternately forward and back. You didn't have to be white to walk like that, but you had to come from the East End of London.

I slid up to him along the cold brass rail of the bar. 'Got any more?'

'You what?'

'Tapes?'

'Oh yeah. Nah. You got the last two. Thanks for the 2p tip.'

He took a long draught of his bitter. I stood there trying to make myself look small and crestfallen, until Tommy looked over his glass at me and realised that I wasn't about to go away. Placing his beer on the bar, he stuck his hands into his zippered black leather bomber jacket and straightened up. He was a big-boned, good-looking man with bad skin and skinny with it, so his backside didn't fit his Levi's, which were a little baggy around the back. His large, round, hazel eyes stared out from under a ridge of bone that was his forehead, and his wide, thick eyebrows almost met in the middle. Where they stopped over the bridge of his slightly crooked nose, they pushed up, so that he always looked as if he didn't understand the question.

'In 'ere, have a look,' he said at last, and ducked down by the bar, snapping open his case. There were about twenty cassettes in there, and none by Carla or Johnny Waits.

'No more Carla Blue, Johnny Waits? I want to get some for someone else,' I said, squatting close enough to smell the soft leather of his jacket.

'Nah. Listen, I'm here next Sunday, and I got a shoe stall down the Roman, Thursdays, might have some with me then. All right, doll?'

'Yeah. All right. Thanks.' I straightened up.

'Want a drink?' he said, clicking the case shut, and looking at my legs.

'I don't drink before . . . Oh hell, why not? I've never met anyone in the music business before,' I said, smiling all the time.

Tommy turned out to be very talkative, about nothing in particular. He said he liked my short, dark hair, my blue eyes and my short skirt, but he was the sort of guy that you'd catch, every now and then, looking slyly at someone else while he spoke to you. He stood a round for a couple of friends at the end of the bar and when they joined us, I left, with his phone number in my pocket.

'It's me brother's gaff, but you can leave a message.'

I went straight home and played the tapes. The reproduction was good, which meant I'd probably got copies from the first batch. That's if they were copies. The albums weren't being launched until Friday. The stores hadn't got them in yet, so Tommy and his team couldn't have bought one from which to make a copy. That's what pirates did. It wasn't any more complicated than that. I listened while I looked at the covers and cases. They could easily have been the real thing. The tapes could have been stolen, literally off the back of a lorry bound for the stores. Tommy said they were the real thing, as any self-respecting street trader would. The artwork was good enough, too.

Carla's voice leapt out clear and sweet on the first track and the notes jabbed at my memories of her. I expected tears to fill my eyes and start down my cheeks, but they didn't come. When the second track began, I got up out of the chair and went into the kitchen where I kept the wine, and poured myself a big cold glassful. The music just wasn't up to it. What I needed was Joni Mitchell singing "Blue".

I ejected Carla after the first side and put Waits into the slot. One or two tracks were as good as any I had heard, but the rest were sub-standard fare hardly good enough to drive down motorways to. These were the out-takes, the ones that hadn't made the earlier albums, and hence they were unreleased. It wasn't as if Ghea had suddenly found a treasure trove in the guy's attic. There were two new ones from 1988. I checked the inside of the sleeve. One called 'Crystal Form' featured a dolphin calling, the other was a mystical floaty number called 'The Channeller'. They'd been recorded in California a few months before he died, presumably in the dawn of a New Age. I reckoned the dolphin had a lot of potential even though it had to work hard against the gongs and tinkling bells coming from the speakers. So did my telephone.

It had been ringing a while before I jumped up to answer it. Every time, I hoped it would be someone telling me that there had been a mistake and that Carla was really alive, that it was someone else that had drowned. Someone I didn't care about. But it was St John, irritated by the delay. They were bringing Carla's body home tomorrow for the funeral and Carla's mother had asked that I be there.

'Meet us at Heathrow check-in at eight a.m. We'll catch the flight to Cornwall from there,' he said, and put the phone down. He made it sound like just another out-of-town gig.

This time I put the headphones on and played the tapes again while I worked my way through a bottle of cold, dry wine and two cheese and tomato sandwiches. At the sober end of the session, I wondered how Tommy had got his tapes and what it would be worth for someone to know, but by the time I got to the dolphin again I'd forgotten about Tommy and had started thinking back to my ex-husband Eddie and me at Sea World. He was living in California now, making money out of computer software. He was a lucky man. He'd never really been caught, not by me or anyone, not in love or in any of his money-making scams. He'd been caught out though, for sure, but it wasn't the same thing.

The music stopped, the bottle was empty and I was back thinking about Carla. The telephone didn't ring again.

'Christ, can you believe that? I sent only one coach, and there must have been five or six trying to turn round in that alley they call a road. We got to have a fucking memorial service, now,' St John said to no one in particular on the way back to the airport.

Dexter and I sat staring out of opposite windows. 'Why don't you get public relations on to it?' I said, and he took the point. No one said another word until we got on the plane.

Mrs Ball had requested a small, private, family funeral, but most of the hundred or so of Carla's fans and press had been in the village most of the night. We arrived in a big black stretch limousine slightly smaller than a coach, and as we edged down the hill, dozens of people were still making their way towards the crowded churchyard. The hearse couldn't pull up close to the church. It had to swing in behind a beige Bedford painted with a huge elastic hot dog and a bottle of tomato ketchup. The car nosed through a group of hefty-looking types who were standing around drinking hot coffee out of white polystyrene cups. As soon as our driver opened the doors, they chucked them aside and came at us armed with cameras and lenses like bazookas.

It took some time, but when the bearers eventually got the casket out, they staggered with it through the crowd like a pantomime horse heading for exit stage left and then right. It took fifteen minutes for them to stumble into the church. The pews were packed. There was no space between the press of people and us. Their breath was in our faces and on our necks and no one knew the words of the hymns. I'd been afraid that the service would be moving, but now I knew it would be nothing like that. I couldn't cry for her here, either. It was all a nothing, an empty ritual. She wasn't there. There was just a heavy box in a cold stone church full of strangers.

'A grain of wheat is a solitary grain of wheat until it falls to the ground and dies, but if it dies, it bears a rich harvest,' said the priest, by way of comfort to an uncomprehending congregation, unbelievers from the urban conurbations. Carla certainly didn't believe in that: that you were better off dead, getting your reward and comfort in heaven. She wanted results in this world, like now, like yesterday. The priest didn't know Carla. To Carla, death was unimaginable. The beyond was not her market. It would be worse than a US tour, worse than being an ex-pat. Anyway, she had been too busy making it to think about death and her reward in heaven.

Outside, the sea mist that had greeted us at the airport was beginning to recede over the cliffs, and the watery, winter sun had started to ooze through the cloud. The golden nameplate on the casket caught the light a little, the only movement but for three wisps of gingery hair blowing back from the priest's bald head as he spoke.

'We therefore commit her body to the ground; earth to earth, ashes to ashes; in sure and certain hope of the Resurrection to eternal life,' he said, and we all stared down at the bright casket in the gloomy pit.

We waited for Mrs Ball to stoop and sprinkle the dirt down on to it, make a start, but someone threw a rose over the heads of St John and Dexter and startled her. It landed with a slight skip and a bounce on the coffin lid, breaking the silence the priest had charmed with his solemn words. Three more followed, and then more. Red roses for a blue lady. I wanted to laugh. Carla would have done. She loved a good cliché. People began leaning over to have a look until the pressure of the crowd began to shift us forward.

I had to lean back hard to stop myself slipping down the moist loose earth at the grave's edge. St John swore as he and Dexter held their arms out to steady themselves, like two policemen creeping along a ledge fifty feet high towards a prospective suicide. It got rougher as the mass of bodies behind the ones at the front started to crush forward.

The whole funeral party would have followed Carla into the abyss if St John hadn't turned and leaned into the crowd like a lineman for the Chicago Bears and managed to bully a small break in the advancing line. 'Geddoudafit. Out of the way . . . move . . . Out of it . . . Move!' he shouted, slapping a few heads, and dragging our shaken little party past the hundreds of pairs of curious eyes towards the car waiting by the graveyard gates.

We were driven slowly to the family home on the outskirts of the village, where we sat for an hour in virtual silence, little plates of vol-au-vents on our laps. Mrs Ball, perched on the edge of her chair, cried into her handkerchief every time she tried to speak.

*

I mentioned the tapes to St John on the flight home because I thought the news would annoy him. I really wanted to spoil his day. Christian Dexter had chosen to sit in gloomy isolation by a window seat on the half-empty aircraft and I sat with St John across the aisle, in the aisle seat. When the stewardess came by, St John leaned over and ordered a large Scotch for himself and a gin and tonic for me.

Leaning back, he undid the one button of his dark jacket and waited for the drinks to come. Despite the expensive, sombre suit, white shirt and black tie, St John lacked true elegance. He cut a fine figure for a hippopotamus, but for a clothes-horse he was simply the wrong shape. His chest was too big and his waist too thick. He had what rugby players call duck's disease, that is, his legs were short and his backside was too close to the floor. He looked tough though, he made sure of that, with his sandy hair cropped to half an inch all round, shaved up, back and sides, to expose a thick neck, belted with tight pinkish folds of muscle that stood out like the ridges of some fleshy spring.

'St John'll kick their asses!' Carla used to say in times of crisis. 'When you sit around that long teak table talking deals and contracts, you don't want no leper-loving St Francis of Assisi giving it all away; you want the meanest son of a bitch in the known universe reading the small print.' St John, the patron saint of bug-squashers, was no St Francis, for sure.

Some said he was insane, but it was arguable whether the outrageous pranks for which he was famous were the actions of a dangerous lunatic or just harmless clowning. He'd actually commandeered a radio station once that had failed to deliver. The story was that he had paid UKR fifteen thousand to plug a début single by Strangeways, a pre-punk heavy metal band. UKR had one unwise DJ, who thought he had better taste than the producer of his show. Unfortunately, taste was not the issue. The DJ didn't deliver the air-time, and lived to regret it. They say the man, who was locked into the same room as St John for three hours, still isn't quite right, though his show is very popular.

I asked Carla why she had picked him.

'I didn't. He picked me. The guys thought he was a bit of a thug but I knew he'd get me what I wanted. With St John, you're talking hype, hype, hype, entrepreneurship, a strong arm, hard knuckles, and hype, hype, hype. He's not scared of going gung-ho right over the top and sticking the flag up someone's bum.'

St John had a history of sticking it to them. He had experience. He pre-dated punk, and when those spiky pogo years sounded the alarm on the somnambulent seventies, he was there acting as commercially as the next pop manager, cultivating his own anti-social, anti-establishment persona. He still had one or two big acts from those days, ones that hadn't self-destructed, but Carla had been the freshest, and the most successful, performer that he had discovered in a long time.

Now he stared out at the clouds through the thick rounded window to his left, shaking his knees back and forth as he sat, chewing constantly at the thumbnail of his right hand. His thumb resembled a lightly cooked sausage, wrinkled, as if it had been grilled and left in the fridge for a couple of days. There was a small ridge of nibbled nail above the cuticle and a huge expanse of gnawed skin above it forming a dome, like the pate of Elmer Fudd's cartoon head. He twitched like a man whose brain was no more than a hyperactive pinball machine, unlike the lean and lanky Christian Dexter, who sat moody and motionless a few seats away on the other side of me.

'Let me tell you about counterfeit tapes,' St John began, once he had downed his golden whisky and exhaled the fumes with a sigh. 'They cost me a lot of money, likewise Ghea and . . . Carla. Well, yes, and Carla. She may be dead, but she's still in business.'

He looked over for my agreement, but I didn't give it. I was remembering the inscription on Carla's nice new marble headstone. Her mother had chosen it.

'Charlotte Ball, the singer, Carla Blue, only beloved

child of Miranda and Charles. Died November 22nd 1989, aged 27 years. For thy sweet love remembered such wealth brings.'

St John couldn't have put it better himself.

'You do understand, don't you? Pirates, bootleggers and counterfeiters are different, OK? A bootlegger does an illicit recording at a concert and then knocks out the tapes for a few quid a time. No royalties for the artists, no percentage for the manager, no return on investment for the record company. Too bad. A pirate gets hold of back catalogue stuff and puts together an album, CD, whatever, or gets a hold of a copy of something that never went out, like Prince's 'Black' album, and sells it. Now . . . most pirates operate in wop countries which have pathetic copyright laws, like Italy or Portugal, and they're not doing anything illegal, unless they sell over here. Still no royalties for the artist, no percentage for the manager, no return on investment for the record company. Too bad. The counterfeiter is something else; he's a real bastard. He walks into a record store, buys a tape, takes it home, slots it into a duplicating machine and reels off hundreds, thousands, of copies. Same thing? No! Worse! Much worse . . . because they're stealing our fucking sales! The others, all they're doing is not paying us our due. These bastards steal sales of our albums as surely as if they'd jumped up and removed them from the back of the proverbial fucking lorry!'

He leaned over me again to catch the stewardess's eye. The trip was just an hour long, but this man didn't want to be caught short without a Scotch. He was so close I could smell his lemon balm cologne and see into his ear, shiny, scrubbed and clean. I turned my face away.

'And we're talking money,' he continued, settling back in the seat and flicking imaginary particles from his trousers. 'The biggest police haul to date was in Glasgow. The geezer had eleven duplicating machines capable of knocking out 20,000 counterfeit tapes a week. What's that mean? Let's work it out. At £3 a time, that's £60,000 a week, £240,000 a month, an annual turnover of £2.7 million – that's more than some record companies fucking *make* in a year! That haul was one-third of the estimated counterfeit audio tape industry! Nearly nine-million-pounds worth! And they wonder why the Chinks are getting out of smack and into this! It's easy money, that's why . . . and we haven't even begun to talk about videos.' His huge thighs swung back and forth, and Elmer Fudd was being gnawed like a dogbone.

I finished my gin and started knocking cubes of ice around the inside of my transparent plastic cup. 'So how did our friend the counterfeiter get these, then?' I said.

Elmer Fudd got a sharp suck and exploded out of St John's mouth. 'Could only be advance copies. I know. I know. Some bastard's going to die for this, and I'm gonna be the one that fucking kills them.' St John stopped twitching and gnawing and folded his hands comfortably over his rounded groin as if the effort of his speech and the comforting possibility of revenge had calmed him down.

'Well, in that case, I won't tell you who's been pushing them out. I think you're crazy enough to do it.'

He waved a hand at me and laughed, as if admiring the cheek of one so young. 'Gedoutofit!' Then his eyebrows turned the look on his face to one that said, 'No, seriously.'

'No, seriously. You're a journo, aren't you? You think this counterfeit scam is a story, yeah?'

'Someone might buy it. Sounds good. Pirates pre-launch Carla's LP, something like that. Nine-million-pound industry – nice feature material, you know.'

'Counterfeiters.'

'The subs'll call them pirates. Better imagery for the reading public.'

'Maybe. But I got something better than that.'

'Oh yes?' I gave the cup of ice another whirl.

'How about . . . Carla Blue's death caused by drug orgy?' he said, leaning forward and grabbing the in-flight magazine.

'She drowned,' I said, while he browsed through the pages.

'I know, but why'd she do a crazy thing like swim in that pool with waves crashing over it? Why did she go down there? The rest of us didn't. She was a smackhead, that's why. Head full of shit.' He turned the magazine upside down in frustration. 'Who's stupid idea is this to print half the pages upside down?'

'One bit's on London for outgoing passengers, the other bit is on the West Country for incoming passengers. She didn't go alone, did she?'

'No. She went with . . . they had a thing together.' He tossed the irritating magazine to one side and nodded lightly, but discreetly, to the other side of the aircraft where Christian Dexter sat staring out of the window at the cumulo-nimbus piled up in the cold sky.

I looked over. She couldn't have done it with him. She couldn't have. What if she did? Maybe she wanted him to do something for her. The cow. I wouldn't put it past her. I closed my eyes for the rest of the trip. So what was bothering me? The thought that it might be the truth, or the thought that it might be a lie?

It wasn't my by-line that ran on the front page of the tabloid dailies the next day. Accompanying the blown-up funeral pictures was the story of Carla's fall from grace. CARLA BLUE DRUG DEATH. STAR IN DRUG HORROR. OVERDOSE KILLED CARLA. HUNDREDS AT FUNERAL OF STAR.

One way or another, the stories were the same. Carla had been high on heroin when she stepped into the pool, and Dexter had tried to save her. There were traces of morphine in her body. Party-goers suggested that she might also have been sniffing cocaine earlier in the evening. The Spanish police were investigating.

St John knew how to place a story. What harm was there in it, he would argue, the girl was dead, but still in business. He still had to do his best for her. But it was a hard week for memories.

Everywhere I turned there was her picture, her name, or

her, preserved in twenty synchronised TV images, half
naked on the new video, gyrating on the screens of every
major record store. Advance copies of the new single taken
from the album, 'Seethru' were in high demand. Coming
soon, the dead Carla Blue. Boomph, up on the satellite,
down, and there you have it, a dual triple-format launch,
worldwide. All the man with the flared nostrils had to do was
press the button, like royalty smashing a champagne bottle
on a new ship.

I had a few calls from reporters offering me money for my
story.

'Georgina Powers?'

'Yes.'

'I'm from the *Sun*. We saw you at the funeral. Could we
do a deal on a story?'

'About what?'

'You were a friend, perhaps you could help us with a
profile?'

'I'm working on a story of my own.'

'Oh, I get it. Come on, do it for us, forget NUJ rates.'

'I'm sure, but no thanks.'

'Suit yourself, love, but you're not in this business for your
health. What's your price?'

'Hey, why don't you just make something up and save
yourself a few bob?'

'Well, fuck you.'

I couldn't tell them anything. What did I know, anyway? I
could tell them she was full of surprises. Into women, into
drugs, into Christian Dexter.

The tabloids went ahead and built a line-by-line
monument to her memory. They analysed her talent, her
mysterious appeal to the young, her wasted life, and the
tragic sickness that undermined her true potential. It was the
least they could do. To die at the height of one's career was
the ultimate sacrifice for wall-space in the hall of fame. But
to die an anti-hero meant she would be sealed in wax. She
would be a perpetual source of mystery, sadness . . . and

good copy. She would never age, and her image never alter. The world could have full strength undiluted Carla Blue for ever.

Every time you turned a dial or a page, drug abuse was the high profile issue: in Carla's beloved phone-ins, in special news analysis reports on the radio and late night TV. In every media discussion, Carla and Johnny Waits's deaths from heroin were mentioned almost in the same breath. Smack, the rock star's way to go. I couldn't believe she had gone so far.

'I want you to take this with me. Share it.' It looked like a mint in her hand.

'What is it?'

'MDMA.'

'Ecstasy?'

'Yeah. Aceeeid. P-P-P-Plenty in the house.'

'Thanks, but no thanks.'

'Why?'

'It's dangerous, isn't it? I thought psychiatrists in the US fed it to schizophrenics, and then banned it.'

'Nah, they used it for mending marriages. Honest. That's 'cos it gives you the horn and makes you really want to be truthful.'

'The truth hurts, Carla.'

'Come on. One hit's not going to kill you. They say you get a sort of out-of-body experience, a great feeling of awareness and perception. Things look the same only much, much nicer. They say afterwards you're kind of bonded to the people you take it with.'

'Oh yeah? Well, I don't want to be bonded with you. You're crazy.'

I should have told her you didn't need hallucinogenic amphetamine to get bonded to someone. Love did it, so did hate. Guilt was a good starter, too. Guilt bonds you together like glue.

Chapter 4

I telephoned Tommy, and the phone rang long enough for me to think there was no one at home.

'Allo?' There was a great deal of background noise.

'I want to speak to Tommy.'

'Who?'

'Tommy,' I shouted against the noise of the pub.

'Tommy who?' It was a man's voice.

'I don't know. Tommy down the market.'

'Yeah?' It was Tommy.

'It's me, Georgina Powers – last Sunday, remember? We had a drink. I bought a couple of tapes.'

'Oh yeah! Sorry, sweetheart. You what? You want come over for a drink?'

'Yeah. Where?' I shouted.

'Salmon and Ball. You know it?'

I knew it. The guy was an East Ender. It wasn't far from home.

The Salmon and Ball was a handsome Victorian pub that stood on the corner of a busy junction in Bethnal Green. It was one of the few in the area that had not been splashed in new cocktail colours and named after a month in the year. Its pea-green, glazed, half-tiled walls gave way to large windows with little frosted squares at the bottom. A hand-painted sign hung above the double door. I pushed through it into a tiled corridor. Two brass-handled doors opened to the left and the right. On the opaque, ornate,

41

bevelled glass the words 'Public' and 'Saloon' were fancily engraved. I opened the door to the large public bar.

Tommy stood by the open hatch of the wooden counter, close to a bright pool table lit up in the smoky darkness at the far end of the bar. He was talking to a dark-haired man in a smart, double-breasted suit. Only Tommy smoked, cupping his hand over the lighted end as he inhaled and withdrew the cigarette from his mouth at one and the same time.

I made my way towards them through the small and noisy gatherings of drinkers. 'Hello, Tommy,' I said.

'Hello, doll.'

Tommy swung his arm behind me to stub out his cigarette and ended up standing close beside me. His well-heeled drinking partner stayed where he was. He was about my height, maybe taller, five nine; as good, if not better, looking than Tommy, but a bit older, say thirty-five, and lightly built. His nose had a dent just under the bridge and he had sharp eyes that moved quickly, almost imperceptibly, between Tommy and myself. I stepped round him to the bar.

'Can I get you gentlemen a drink?' I said, turning my head and holding a ten-pound note out for the attention of the glossy blonde barmaid in the short pink skirt and top. Her breasts ballooned out at the front, so her centre of gravity fell way beyond her pastel winkle-picker toes. She started to walk towards me.

Tommy stood there with his mouth slightly open, but the man in the dark suit was quicker. 'I'll get these, love,' he said, gently placing his gold-ringed manicured hand on my arm and steering me firmly away from the bar.

I knew that it was never going to work, not in this pub, in this neck of town. My ten-pound note would remain intact for the whole evening, but at least I'd let them know that I was used to being out on my own. I noticed that Tommy's friend didn't pay. I took a cool swallow of the icy aromatic gin and smiled. 'I thought that number you gave me was your brother's place, Tommy.'

He laughed, and offered me a cigarette. 'Er . . . George—ina, meet the landlord, my brother Tony.'

'Oh, I'm sorry.' I smiled again, this time stretching out my hand.

He took it firmly in his warm, dry palm. ' 'S'OK. A pleasure.'

'This gorgeous gel's chasing me round for me tapes, Tony. Ain't it always the way?'

Tony didn't look that interested until I put Tommy right.

'Well, I am . . . and I'm not, Tommy.' Suddenly I had their joint unsmiling interest. 'I'll be straight with you. The tapes are a good price and it's nearly Christmas, but I thought, with your . . . contacts . . . you could do something for me.'

Their eyes said go-to-hell, and only Tommy said, 'Oh yeah?'

I dug into my shoulder-bag and brought out a tape in a clear case. 'The unreleased Carla Blue,' I said, handing it to Tommy. 'It's a collection of songs she did before she joined Ghea. I think they're better than anything she did with them. Better than "Seethru". You can't buy it. Mine's probably the only one in existence. It was my friend Carla's, the late Carla Blue.'

The minds of Tommy and Tony were as one, but it was Tony who did the talking. 'You could go legit to get that done.'

'I have no money to pay up front, no distribution, no intention of paying royalties, I just want a working asset, and a little revenge.'

'Fair enough.'

I was relieved. Tommy's brother's laconic way with words meant that I didn't have to remember too many lies. I tipped my chin up and blew smoke up above their heads. I hoped it looked nonchalant. 'You know, I'd really like to know how you got your hands on those tapes before they'd even reached the shops.'

Tommy's face was blank, but his eyes widened enough to

43

show the white round his irises and take his quizzical eyebrows skywards. I didn't take his hint, and carried on. 'You know, the ones, "Seethru" and "The Unreleased Johnny Waits". I mean, they'll be released this Friday. They're not even in the stores yet.'

Tony was looking straight at Tommy, who started to shrug his shoulders and open his hands out. He had the look of a boy in deep trouble. 'I sold a few at Camden Lock, Sunday. Tony.'

'I told you after, not before.' His mouth had gone viciously small. He turned to me. 'What do you want to know for?'

'No. Nothing. Nothing, really. Just curious. I'm sorry. I can mind my own business. Let's get back to my tape. I want to know if you can deliver, and how much.'

'We got to check it out first, but say, four maybe six thousand a week. We can ride the hype for her new album now.'

Four to six thousand at £2 a go. £12,000 a week. This man was in the bulk side of the business. 'That's incredible! What can I expect?'

'Ten per cent.'

'For you? That's generous. I'll take it.'

He looked unsmilingly at me, but Tommy had started to grin.

'OK, guys, start again. I want fifty per cent.'

'Thirty,' said Tony.

'Thirty-five.'

'OK.'

We shook hands. He nodded politely and pocketed the tape before ordering another round of drinks. Tommy was the first to speak. He wagged a nicotine-stained finger at me and flicked open his packet of Marlboro with his thumb for me to take another. 'You're a bit of a dark horse, aincha? Here's me thinking you're after me body, and . . . '

'Boxing out your class, old son,' said his brother, managing to pay me a compliment that kicked his brother in the metaphorical crotch.

Tommy's face told me he was sick of the big brother treatment. He felt on safe ground. Women were obviously his department. 'Oh, do me a favour, Tone. I know about class, I know . . . let's say more'n you ever will. But I keep it shut.' He touched his yellow finger to his lips and turned to me. 'I don't kiss and tell. You can trust me, doll.'

We laughed, and Tony nodded, unimpressed. 'Are you staying for another drink, Georgina?'

He had Tommy's hazel eyes, but harder, shrewder, creased a little at the edges, not from squinting into the light but from the many harsh little assessments he made every day. He was making one now, and unlike his brother's, his eyebrows stayed put, like the whole upper part of his face was dead.

'No, thank you all the same. I've got to go. But here's my number. Just in case.' I scribbled a note on the back of an old business card and handed it to him. 'Can you give me yours? I don't want to call the payphone again.'

'Sure,' he said, picking up a small square beer-mat. I handed him my ballpoint pen. He wrote down the figures quickly and handed me the mat.

'Levi. Tony Levi,' I read.

'That's right,' he replied with his back to me as he walked to the phone to call a cab.

I sat back in the car, feeling very pleased with myself. Tony Levi, pub landlord, tape pirate, and what else? Handmade suits, Swiss cotton shirts, soft leather shoes and gold rings on his pinkies – a man who thought well of himself. He bossed his brother, and Tommy didn't like to cross him, or rather, he liked to cross him but he didn't like him finding out. Tommy had tried something on for himself but it hadn't turned out too badly. It looked like Tommy was used to that.

'How much?' I said, leaning in towards the minicab driver.

'Mr Levi pays,' he said, and gunned the Merc round the block.

St John had left a message on my answering machine. The police, together with members of the British Phonographic Institute's Anti-Piracy Unit, were going to raid Camden Lock market on Sunday morning, and Ghea were having a party on Saturday night. I could go to both if I wanted to. The first thing I did was pick up the phone and call the number on the beer-mat. Tony wanted to know how I knew about the raid and I told him I had friends in the business. That was all I had to say.

Ghea's Christmas party was worse than I had thought it would be. It was at one of those nightclubs that rich people were supposed to patronise, so what you got were expense-account out-of-towners and escorts on the nights that the club wasn't hired out to commerce and industry. Keith had telephoned as well to say he'd meet me there, otherwise I wouldn't have gone. He said that we should talk. I knew what we'd be talking about. Carla. It was time I talked to somebody about her, somebody who might be able to share a few memories with me, say that he missed her, explain how she'd ended up taking hard drugs, and feel sorry, something like that. I wanted to talk to someone who wasn't making money out of her.

Two thick-set bouncers in tuxedos checked out my invitation, and pointed me down the red carpet to the dark interior of the club where fifty or so guests mingled in the softly lit gloom away from the spangled oval of the dance floor. It was far too early to dance.

A black waiter stood silently beside me with a silver tray weighed down with gently bubbling champagne. I took a glass and looked around for Keith. I couldn't see him. John St John caught sight of me from the other side of the bar and lifted his hand to wave me over. I forced a smile, and cursed Keith. Where was he?

St John was with Christian Dexter and a tall beautiful redhead who wore a gripping black halter-neck cocktail dress and long dark gloves to great effect. She stood silently

46

between the two men, twisting an empty glass round and round in her hand. I recognised her from somewhere. She was no one I knew, but someone I had seen. She might have been a singer or an actress, but I wasn't sure.

'Good evening, Georgina,' said St John, bringing me to his side with another wave. ' 'Course you know Chris. This is his wife, Cheryl LeMat. Cheryl, Georgina Powers, a good friend of Carla.'

Ms LeMat smiled, turning up her mouth sharply at the edges, but I didn't see it in her wide, wet, indifferent green eyes. Cheryl LeMat. She was a model. I remembered straight away. Cheryl LeMat. It was her. Cover of *Vogue*, *Sports Illustrated*, you name it. It was a few years ago, but she still looked good with those legs that went on for ever and that curtain of hair all down her back. I'd never seen her eyes like that, though, with pupils as dark and empty as whirlpools. I wondered if she knew about Dexter and Carla, or if she cared.

'Pleased to meet you,' I said, and she nodded but said nothing, so I continued, hoping to make a little small talk that would crack the permafrost. 'Didn't you . . . '

'Use to be famous?' she said.

'Well, aren't you still?' I said, wishing I'd kept my mouth shut.

'Well, let's say I don't work so much nowadays.' She snapped the reply at me and looked away, still twisting her glass.

'You could get as much work as you liked if you just got your act together and got out of bed,' Dexter muttered, and drained his glass.

'Trouble is, Dexter dear, there are no agency bookers like you any more. You know how a girl relies on her booker, and I can't seem to find one with that personal touch.'

The conversation was about modelling, but it wasn't. What we had here was a nasty little skirmish in the battle between the sexes, and so I turned to St John to try my small-talk out on him. I tried to keep it less controversial than my opening gambit to Ms LeMat.

'How'd the launch go?' I said.

He was busting to answer. 'Unbelievable. Unbe-fucking-lievable. We hired out those swimming baths. The Porchester. "Seethru". Water. Get it?' He jogged my arm just to make sure that I did.

'I get it, and given the circumstances, a trifle tasteless, don't you think?' I said.

St John obviously hadn't thought, and from their faces, the others hadn't either. The three exchanged glances until he spoke up for them all. 'No one picked up on that. It doesn't matter anyway. Both albums were advance sell-outs – they'll be number one and two for Christmas. "Seethru" sold 20,000 today alone. It's another "Thriller", and CBS can kiss my ass.' He laughed like a man who had just won a national lottery, and clapped Dexter on the back.

Dexter didn't laugh, and Cheryl LeMat looked at St John as if she'd just spat him out. St John shrugged off the force of our combined disapproval and shoved Dexter playfully on the chest.

'C'mon, you miserable bastard! Hey, listen . . . Georgina's the one that found those tapes, Chris. She bought some at Camden Lock. You and her'd get on. She's a computer journalist, writes about that high-tech stuff . . . ' He tapped his finger to his temple. I could either be a genius or a lunatic in his book. 'Yes, Chris's your man, Georgina. Tap-tap-tapping on those keyboards, one of them wire-heads, aren't you, mate?'

St John started laughing again, but Dexter still ignored him, but this time for a different reason. He and Cheryl LeMat were looking past us, standing tensely together. I glanced over my shoulder. A rather large, balding man was standing at the foot of the stairs. He stood with his legs apart, planted firm on fallen arches, pudgy hands on hips.

'The bastard . . . ' St John said, as the man grabbed a glass from a tray and scanned the room like a snorting bull surveying horses in a bullring. He was not alone. There was a broad black man with a severely shaved head bringing up the rear. The two made their way to a cliquey gathering of the music press and came away after ten minutes, laughing hugely. They started towards us.

'Mikey! Domey! You fat bastard! How are ya!' St John stepped forward, hand outstretched.

I knew who it was, now. Mike Dome of the Mike Dome Agency. They both shook hands like they were pumping a well. Dome leaned over and gently kissed the beautiful cheek of the lovely Cheryl. She smiled. Not a big white smile for the cameras, but a little, puckered, pinched one for him.

Dome turned to face her husband. There was no handshake, and certainly no peck on the cheek. 'How's it goin', Dexter my old chum?'

'OK.' Dexter looked like a man who'd caught a whiff of something on his shoe.

'Aw, c'mon, better than OK, better than OK! Hey, bet you can't believe your fucking luck . . . '

'What?'

'Two dead stars on your hands in two years. Hey!' Dome clapped his hands together with a sweaty little pop. 'Bingo!'

St John pushed his hand up to Dome's shoulder and, a little nervously, persisted with the locker-room bonhomie. 'Hey! Hey, Mikey . . . Domey . . . Cool it, you crazy bastard, what's goin' on?'

The broad black man with the savage haircut gently took St John's hand away, Elmer Fudd and all, like a good wife picking a loose thread from her husband's suit. If Dexter was afraid, he didn't show it. People had begun to notice the scene. The gathering of the music press edged a little closer in a many-legged clump.

Dome shoved his finger up at Dexter's face. 'I kicked your ass in court with Johnny, you cold bastard. You're damn lucky he up and died on you so you could pay me off. But you got lucky twice. I say you're getting careless, Dexter, very careless. What you say?'

'I say you're a pig, Dome, with no respect for anyone.'

'Yeah? Well, this pig is going to take his cute little piglets away from the nasty old bacon-maker. You like that idea, bigshot?'

'Get out of my face, Dome.' Dexter was speaking through his teeth, looking down at Dome, who was already turning to leave the party with his quiet friend.

St John had grasped Cheryl LeMat's elbow, squeezing it. I saw her shut her mouth tight and blink her eyes hard shut before opening them to look behind me to somewhere else in the room. She smiled a little nervously, but not at me.

Merry Christmas to one and all, I thought, stepping smartly back to avoid being thrust aside and colliding with a group of onlookers behind. Someone goosed me. It was Keith, in a suit.

'Hi,' he grinned, showing a fine display of even teeth. 'How're ya doin'?' he enquired, slipping his hand round my back and moving me away from the frosty little trio that now stood behind me. 'Like the floor show?'

'Charming. But tell me, how come you were invited?'

'Mr City.'

'You are?'

'Well, no, about three of us write the page. I mean I can't be everywhere it's at.'

'What happened to the beachwear?'

'Give me a break, that was two years ago! I told you I'm Mr City now.'

'Did you hear what he said?' I said, picking up another glass of champagne from a passing tray.

'About his piglets? Great, wasn't it?'

'Yes, but what did he mean?'

Keith brushed back the heavy weight of his dark hair and felt around in his suit for his cigarettes like a man whose pocket had just been picked. I snapped open my black clutch-bag and offered one of mine. He did the same routine for his lighter.

'Look. Ghea's looking to go public next year. That's why we've got this restrained little function here. The music dos are usually, how shall I put it, a little funkier? Now Dome is

50

an animal. You think St John eats raw meat? Well, the guy's a vegan compared to Dome. Personally, I think Mike is a good sort for all his ball-breaking business technique and, oh, those manners!'

'Why the scene?'

Keith motioned us away to a safe corner by the heavily draped window. 'Dome wants to queer Dexter's pitch. He's been making noises about getting his two megagroups – the Dudes and the Nodding Dogs, both rock solid bands – out of Ghea. I'm not sure how the lads themselves feel about that, but Mike knows their contracts are coming up for renewal and that the deal Ghea's suggesting isn't too sweet. Ghea wants to manage them as well, like it did Waits. It wants a few more people tied up in-house. Dome has a problem if the bands decide to go against him, for the sake of keeping the recording contract. St John probably has his eye on them as well.'

'You can't just steal a manager's acts, can you?'

'Well, you can if they don't want to stay, but it causes big, big legal problems if the manager puts up a fight. Dome's bands have been around for ten years and are two of the biggest selling bands in the world. He won't want to lose them.' Keith patted his pockets for another cigarette. I was about to snap open my bag again when he raised one hand and stuck the other inside his jacket. 'I have this problem with keys and sodding pieces of paper.' He offered me one of his long cigarettes and a light from a blue see-through lighter that shot fire like a flamethrower.

'More to it than that, of course. Dome and Dexter go way back . . . to Johnny Waits. Dexter discovered him back in the seventies and managed him, got him gigs, paid his bills, all but wiped the guy's . . . er . . . nose. Just before he made it, Waits up and went with the Mike Dome Agency, which was making a lot of noise then, squeezing amazing million-plus advances out of record companies for one and all. There was litigation – Dexter came off worst. It was a shame. Dexter did all the groundwork and pumped money

51

into Waits, but it was Dome who really broke Waits internationally. Tough, but true. Dexter got out of the business after that. Want some mince pies?'

I shook my head and looked over to see if I could see Dexter's blond head in the crowd. I couldn't. I could see Cheryl LeMat bending her head over and talking to St John. She looked angry and upset.

'When did he join Ghea?'

'Oh . . . no. Dexter founded Ghea ten years ago. It's his company, one of the biggest independents in the country now. Going public could net him £300 million, maybe more.'

Keith managed to cram a whole mince pie into his mouth in just one and a half bites. I had to wait. 'Mmmm . . . The story doesn't end there. He got Waits back with a management and recording contract, and they made it with "Here's Johnny" – and it's still in the charts. But shit, the legal battle was horrendous. Waits wanted to go, but Dexter had to pay Dome two million.'

'That's why he made the dig about dead stars?'

Keith came a little closer. I could smell fresh pastry and cigarettes on his breath as he whispered. 'Mike Dome knows where Dexter's goolies are. You see . . . Waits and Dexter were lovers. I mean it. Old sex machine Waits was an out-and-out iron, but Dexter here is a . . . duallist . . . shall we say. Carla told me. Personally, all I know is that Cheryl LeMat is number one wife and I haven't heard of any monkey business to date. Well, look at her, if a woman could get a man to go straight, she could. But get this . . . When Waits OD'd, Dexter was with him. Dexter took Waits to hospital the night he died. Think about it.' Keith pulled down the corner of one eye with his finger.

I put my still full plate of prawn-stuffed vol-au-vents down on the table by the window. 'He was with Carla, too, you know,' I said, as Keith brushed the crumbs from his jacket.

'Yeah.'

One dies in Dexter's arms, the other just out of reach. To lose one may be regarded as a misfortune, to lose both looks like carelessness. Just like the man said. I must have looked depressed, because Keith put his arm round me and gave me a comforting squeeze.

'What say we go some tequila slammers at Los Locos? I'm sick of this Yuletide fare and I could piss on these animals here. Let's see the girl off good and proper!' He took my arm and we sallied out together in search of killer cocktails, hot chili and tortilla chips. 'Call me David,' he said, as we stepped into a cab.

'Don't be ridiculous,' I replied.

At midnight, we were still at the bar.

'I've done something . . . very naughty, Keith,' I mumbled against his shirt.

'Not yet you haven't . . . Arf! Arf!' he said, snorting over his tenth bowl of corn chips.

'Very funny. No, really, I have.'

'Well, my little cactus flower, you can tell the boy David here all about it, he's very understanding . . . and discreet. Tweet, tweet . . . OK? Ready for blast-off?'

'OK!'

Our hands jerked out and grasped the tall glasses while Keith rang a little bell on the bar. We flung our heads back, emptied the tequila at speed down our open throats and just as the burning liquid hit our stomachs, we threw our heads forward and slapped the bar hard with the open palms of our hands and yelled out loud. 'Wh . . . Who . . . Whoaw!'

My head was buzzing with mescal and the barman was getting taller and more distant at one and the same time. I decided not to speak for a little while, and picked up a chip to chew. The crumbs seemed to explode and multiply in my mouth. Keith's eyes were watering.

'Ever had it with a worm?' he said.

'Possibly.'

'In the bottle. The Mexicans stick a worm in a bottle of mescal and you have to eat the worm to prove your manhood.'

'Keith, you may not have noticed, but I don't have to prove my manhood. You eat the worm, and if you get a hard-on, drink the rest of the bottle.'

The barman said he didn't have a bottle with a worm in it. I think Keith looked relieved.

'Tell me something about Carla,' I said, corn-chip crumbs filling my mouth.

'What?'

'Who'd she love? Did she love anyone?'

'Herself.'

'Mmm . . . Did you love her?' I prodded Keith's arm, and he picked up a few more chips and started munching.

'Yeah, I did, I suppose. She was a mate, not always a good one, but that's how it is, isn't it?'

'I can't believe she had a thing with Dexter.'

'Yeah? Who said that?'

'St John.'

Keith rolled his eyes upwards. He looked about ten years old, fawn freckles on his pale skin, shiny dark hair flopping over his face, his white shirt baggy and creased, unevenly rolled-up sleeves. He turned towards the barman, who had bent to whisper in his ear. 'Time to go, Georgie. I'll pick up the tab.'

'No, I . . . insist!' I said, fumbling with my chequebook, wishing I had some cash.

'It's on expenses. This is essential research for Mr City,' he replied, stuffing the book back into my crushed bag.

I leaned on the bar and tapped him on the shoulder. 'You didn't answer me.'

He was distractedly patting his pockets for a cigarette. An empty cellophane-wrapped packet lay crumpled by the cluttered ashtray. I pointed to my bag. 'He's got to be lying,' he said, after we'd lit up. I raised my eyebrows and inhaled. I already knew the answer to my next question.

'Why?'

'Carla was into chicks. You know that. One in particular, as far as I know.' Keith was staring right into my eyes now as the smoke drifted over our heads.

I shrugged. 'Why'd he lie?'

'Perhaps he made an assumption. He wasn't screwing her; he thought Dexter was, but maybe he was right. Maybe Carla took on Dexter to get her way with something . . . sounds like our girl. But that's not what bothers me in this little story. What bothers me is the dope they found in her. Carla smoked a bit, she might even have dropped a tab for fun, or sniffed some toot. But she wasn't out to be Janis Joplin. She didn't have those sorts of problems. You'd have to go some to OD on the stuff she took on a regular basis.'

I couldn't imagine anyone screwing Carla. If there was any screwing to be done, Carla would be doing it. Funny how some men said that, even Keith, who knew her. But Keith was right that Carla didn't – hadn't – liked the hard stuff. But what did we know? People changed. I knew that. They always tried to adapt to new and hostile environments.

'She drowned, then,' I said.

'Think about it. If she was on some sort of cocaine spree, she would have felt good enough to swim the Atlantic, or at least give a good impression that she could. But they say she just lay on her back and floated away.'

'The wave took her.'

'Oh yeah.'

'St John said she was on horse.'

Keith looked surprised. 'Smack? He said that? Well, he'd know, I suppose. He'd definitely know that, being on the tour and all that. I know it was in the paper, but it could have been her first time. Think about it. The stuff could've been too strong, or too pure. That's how you OD.' He shook his head, and took the last corn chip.

Chapter 5

I almost threw the free-sheet in the bin, but the headline caught my eye. The drugs scene was starting to hold some fascination for me.

SPIKED HEROIN KILLED TRADER

The brother of local pub landlord was found dead at his home in Bow on Sunday having taken a lethal cocktail of scouring powder and heroin.

Police believe that the man, a market trader, was the victim of unscrupulous drug-pushers operating the area.

Twenty-eight-year-old Thomas Vittorio Levi of 37A Abbey Road, Bow, was poisoned by an intravenous injection of sodium hypochlorite powder – household bleaching and scouring powder – that had been mixed, or 'cut', with his heroin supply, according to post mortem evidence revealed yesterday.

Detective Sergeant Michael Powell of Bow Road police station said that it was unlikely that Mr Levi had knowingly injected himself with poison and that, because of its colour and consistency, it could possibly have been passed off as heroin.

Detective Sergeant Powell warned other drug-users in the area . . .

Thomas Vittorio Levi. Tommy. I folded the paper twice, so

the story was the only thing I could see. I couldn't think straight. Had he really been a junkie? I read the story again, and then the telephone rang.

'Hi there!' It was Keith. 'Hi, you OK?'

'Yes. I'm OK.'

'Fancy lunch?'

'Um, I dunno . . . '

'What's up? You sound down.'

'Keith, I've got something to tell you. Remember I said I'd been naughty?'

'No. When?'

I explained to Keith what I had done with the tape and to whom I had given it. I had thought that he might be very angry; but he was only a little.

'Wait a minute . . . This means you're breaching my copyright and Mick's? You little cow! Christ, I wish I had thought of that!'

'Look, we'll split it, if I ever get the money. But that's not the point now. Things have taken a turn for the worse.' I told him about Tommy.

'You think this Tony guy'll renege on the deal now that his brother's dead?'

'I'm not sure. I don't know. He may not want to carry on right now.'

'Play it cool. Perhaps he'll call you.'

'There's something else. It might be nothing, but Tommy Levi had "Seethru" and "The Unreleased Johnny Waits" on his stall a week before they were released by Ghea.'

Keith started to laugh. 'You mean he beat Ghea to the launch?'

'Yes. Don't ask me where he got the advance copies from, though. Tony didn't know about it either, and he definitely looks like the one who called all the shots in that relationship. The situation got a bit tense, to say the least, when he found out. He wanted them sold after the launch, to mop up demand, I suppose.'

'And selling them before the launch is a bit like waving a

flag with 'this is hooky gear' writ large. Mind you, lots of people get their hands on promo copies. The record companies send them out. I've probably got some somewhere. Interesting. Lunch?'

I looked at my trusty hammerbeat Swatch. Eleven in the morning, and I still had my dressing-gown on. Two days' worth of dirty pans and dishes lay stacked in the kitchen sink. 'Yes, why not?'

'What's your favourite?'

'L'Escargot. Soho's finest.'

'You got it. One o'clock. OK? See you.'

Thomas Vittorio Levi. No radio requiem for him. No classics to play to the public. No eulogy to a wasted young life. I knew I should call Tony, say that I'd seen the paper. But it was hard knowing where to start with him. I thought that I could, perhaps, ask how our little venture was progressing and then say that I'd read about Tommy in the paper. He'd see through that.

I went into my bedroom, where the once smart peach-coloured furnishings were rumpled, crumpled and dusty. It was claustrophobic in there. I slid the sash down for some cold grey morning air, and the hum of traffic rumbled up on the draught. No sunshine today. It looked like rain. Heavy clouds hung around the tall buildings that dwarfed the little lines of houses that had remained from what had covered this area before. Tommy hadn't been far from this place when he died. I bet his mother had lived in a house like one of those and brought up her kids there. He probably lived in a council flat now and Tony probably had a spread in Essex. I tried to remember what Tommy looked like, and all I could see were his quizzical eyebrows. He didn't look like a junkie. He was a bit thin, but what did that mean? So was I. I couldn't understand why pushers would want to kill their customers. Rip them off, maybe, but kill them? How was that good for business? Perhaps he'd stepped on someone's toes. He did that a lot. His brother's. Ghea's.

I turned away from the window, slid my dressing-gown off

and threw it onto the unmade bed. I opened a few drawers and shut them again, opened the wardrobe door and shoved the wire hangers to one side like beads on an abacus. Then I turned and walked out of my bedroom to the telephone. Curiosity was shoving me in the back. If I didn't call Tony, I wouldn't enjoy my lunch. I had a feeling I wasn't going to enjoy it anyway from the anxious feeling in the pit of my stomach. Naked but for a Dallas Cowboys T-shirt, I called him.

'Hello, Tony, it's Georgina. I've just read about Tommy, I'm so sorry.' I was gabbling. Why was I speaking so fast?

'You don't have to worry.' His voice was steady, hard, under control.

'I'm not worried. I said I was sorry.'

'I heard.'

Then silence. I couldn't think what else to say. I couldn't think what he meant. Worry? Why worry when you could panic? My voice hid in my throat.

He spoke first. 'You know Tommy's flat?'

'Well, no . . . Yes! It's 37A Abbey Road.'

'No, you don't know. They got it wrong. Tommy lives at 39A.'

He was testing me. Why was he testing me? The paper's account, and therefore the police account, of Tommy Vittorio Levi's death had not met with the satisfaction of his brother, that's why. Tony Levi was padding quietly along the warm trail of the killers.

The next question was one I hardly dared ask, but I did anyway. 'Tony, was Tommy really a junkie?'

'He was a pusher.'

'I – I didn't know that. The paper said . . . '

'He weren't no grass.'

'No, it didn't say that,' I said gently. 'I'm sorry, why did you say that?'

More silence. I felt suddenly self-conscious of my nakedness under the short T-shirt as if his hard, critical, unflinching eyes were upon me.

'Ajax. Scouring powder. They give it to grasses, cut the smack with it instead of talc or baby laxative.'

'What?'

'Smack. Heroin,' he said.

'I know that. I don't understand the rest.'

'No one sells pure heroin. It's cut or mixed with something that looks similar. It's diluted all down the line by every dealer in the distribution chain. The junkie probably gets two per cent purity in his bag. If someone is a grass, a snitch, they cut the smack with Ajax. It kills you. No one likes a grass.'

'Oh, my God!'

'Yeah, well, he don't know the half of it.'

Yes, what would God know that Tony Levi didn't? I tugged at the back of my T-shirt to bring it further down my legs.

'I – I can't believe this has happened. Do the police have any idea . . .?'

'Don't think so. By the way, the gear is ready. We'll start outing them now, not in Camden. The filth are all over the place.'

'What do you think of the tape?'

'Crap. But what do I know? My idea of a good song is "Satisfaction". Most kids today've never heard of it.'

When I'd put the receiver down I tried to remember his voice. It was tough and toneless. There wasn't a wobble of emotion when he spoke of his brother. Call me sentimental, but I find death, at the very least, disconcerting. Tony sounded as if he would be punishing Tommy's killers, not for Tommy's death, but for a perceived slight against himself.

It was on my mind as I picked at my grilled goat's cheese through its nest of curly endive. Keith poured the cold house white into my glass and kept talking.

'What do you think of it round here now? I mean, look at it. Soho just isn't a cheap night out for clubbers any more. Look around us. Where's the sleaze? It's too upmarket, more expensive than Paris, for God's sake. It's got so bad people are going to the suburbs. Where do you go nowadays?'

'Nowhere. No stamina. I'm slowing up as I approach the big O.'

'You twenty-nine?'

'Very gallant, Keith. Three years to go, actually.'

' 'S'OK. I like older women.'

'How old are you?'

'Twenty-four.'

'Hardly make it as a toy boy, dearie.'

Keith just grunted and began his lunch of grilled calf liver. Half-way through, the conversation swung round to rock heroes, the dead ones.

'It's a typical cycle, it's how these cult heroes are created. Look at them all: Buddy Holly, Otis Redding . . . er . . . who else?'

'Jim Morrison.'

'Yeah, him too . . . Hendrix, Janis Joplin, Waits . . . '

'Sid Vicious.'

'No . . . No, be serious. But hang on . . . Yes! Even that moron.'

'Maybe, but don't be too harsh on him. I quite liked his version of "My Way" played really loud, charming interpretation of the lyric, almost satirical.'

'Yeah, but I bet he didn't know that. He just liked to talk dirty. Anyway, never mind him, what was I saying?'

'It's a cycle,' I said.

'Oh yes. It's a cycle. The first records are untypical, not mainstream, but good, but not that different, just a little different. Then, for a few years, they make great records that don't sell too well, then for a few more years they carry on working at what they have been doing all along, but start getting the credit for it. Then – success, sweet success, recognition, acclaim – then the plane crash, or the drugs overdose, usually one or t'other.'

'What about Carla?'

'Same thing. No, really, the same thing . . . ' Keith waved his fork to make a point, ' . . . only compressed into a couple of years. Substitute months for years.'

My mind was beginning to stray. If I was working, what would I be doing now? Having lunch in this restaurant, probably, with someone just like Keith in full flow. It had begun to rain outside, dulling the glow of the bright and busy sea-green brasserie. I thought about Carla's unsatisfactory new album that was riding high in the charts.

'What'd you think of "Seethru"?'

Keith chewed the creamy offal, swallowed, and shrugged. He sipped at his wine and didn't answer.

'What's wrong with it?' I said.

'Over-produced. M-O-R.'

'It isn't that bad.'

Keith looked over at me, a little supercilious smile on his lips, his blue eyes gazing at me knowingly, as if we both knew something, as if we both knew why I would want to defend her. My cheeks reddened, infuriatingly. I was angry, but he was bound to interpret the hot glow in my face as embarrassment, it fitted with his little secret.

He spoke before I could. 'It ain't that good either. Come on. It's formula stuff. They've manufactured what we used to do, for the masses. Our stuff was never for the masses, it was for crazy kids in clubs, who didn't give a monkey's about chart hits. A chart hit is death – no exclusivity, you see. We were fucking good too, original. "Seethru" isn't original at all.'

I put my fork down and stopped eating. 'You weren't so hip in the Sweat Box when Dexter signed up Carla and dumped you. Both of you looked like you'd won the pools and someone had forgotten to post the coupon. Come off it! Commercial success means appealing to the masses. You would have killed for a contract with Ghea then.'

Keith held up his hands in surrender, then dropped his right hand, pressing and tapping his forefinger vigorously down on the table as he made each point. 'OK, you're right, but you can still fight for your ideas. After all, they buy you because they like your ideas. You've got to stick with what you believe in. You don't let them fuck you over completely. Let's face it, Carla didn't put up much of a fight, did she? Like she didn't put up much of a fight for us. What she wanted was her picture over everything, not to mention the cash. And who could blame her, huh?'

'You'd have done the same if it was a choice of you or them,' I said.

'Maybe now, but not then. I valued friendship then.'

I took out my irritation on the wrinkled olives scattered like rabbits' pellets in the side salad. He was right. She'd been a pushover. They had packaged her in a big pink bow for "Seethru" and that was what I didn't like about the album. There was not much left of the Carla I knew there. Keith topped up my glass.

'So what about you?' I said. 'You didn't even try to stick with it, did you? For your art.'

Keith took another swallow of wine, tucked his fallen napkin round his neck, and blew out his cheeks. His tie was loose, his dark hair adrift again. 'Yeah, well. I suppose I thought I'd never get that close again. Carla Blue and Big were perfect together. Once she'd split us up, we were less than the sum of the parts, know what I mean? One thing, though. Carla didn't do that early stuff herself. Mick, he wrote most of that stuff, you know. He was the producer, not Carla. And the image, the image that's selling a million? That was my idea. Big and Carla Blue were my idea. But people got carried away with her magic. Ghea bought that magic. They may have thought they were buying more, but that was it.' He shrugged, tipped up the empty bottle of wine and kept on talking as he looked around for the waitress. 'Mind you, you got to hand it to her, she worked at it and made it really something, something different. Remember James Dean? Who said it . . . '

'I don't know, and . . . '

'Dennis Hopper. Like Dennis Hopper said about James

Dean: with one hand he was saying screw you, and with the other, help me. Carla was a bit like that. Difficult, vulnerable. Have you noticed the pictures they keep using? With the chiffon? Soon people will say Carla Blue as soon as they see the eyes, lips, chiffon and little cupcakes – that's all she'll be, an icon, one that says strong female, says weak girl, says leave me alone, says help me, says youth, says energy, and finally, says here is that certain intangible sexual feeling. Her death and all its tragic context just stimulates yearning for all those things, those things that were snatched away. Face it. She's not our Carla any more, but a commodity image to be bought and sold on the open market. Those clever bastards know that, and they're going to clean up.'

He cleared the last remnants of sauce from his plate with a piece of roll. I wasn't enjoying my lunch, not the conversation, or the food, or the wine. I was agitated. It was as if a million little insects were nibbling at my skin. I let my fork clatter on to my plate, crushed my napkin and dropped it on my side plate.

'Have I upset you?' said Keith, a little taken aback.

I put my elbow on the table and rubbed my hand across my forehead. With my eyes closed, life seemed a little better. 'No. It's not you. You're right. I'm just a bit . . . upset, what with one thing and another.'

'You mean Carla.'

I gritted my teeth and whispered harshly through them. 'Stop being so damned understanding! What do you want from me? I did not have an affair with her. She was not my lover. She was my friend. Isn't that enough? I loved her as a friend and I want people to grieve for her as a person. I want to grieve for her as a person and not like I've just lost a pair of my favourite designer jeans!'

Keith maintained a humble silence for a while before the waitress came. I said 'No' to more wine and ordered two espresso coffees for us. We sat in silence until she came back.

'I'm sorry,' he said, his blue eyes scanning my face. I looked away as my eyes filled with hot tears. Keith began desperately patting and thrusting his hands in his pockets for a handkerchief. I got my own and started to laugh. He laughed, too, with relief, and raised a packet of cigarettes in the air instead of the handkerchief. He didn't say anything more. We sat together quietly smoking his cigarettes, Mr City and me. By the third cup of coffee, I started talking, more to myself than Keith.

'I phoned Tony. He checked me out all right. He didn't buy the story in the paper. Apparently that sort of cocktail is delivered to junkies or pushers who grass. Tommy was a pusher but no grass, so Tony says. But I don't know, it's not right, Tommy dying like that. There's something weird about that.'

'Well, you're a journalist, aren't you? Find out.'

'Just like that? I haven't written a word in anger for more than two years.'

Keith gave me a look which suggested that I was swinging the lead. 'Well, you know what they say, it's like riding a bike. Once you learn . . . '

I nodded. ' . . . You never forget. I'm not that bothered, though.'

'I don't believe that. You're nosy. Why'd you buy those tapes? Why'd you really take that tape of ours down to those guys. For money? I don't believe that either. You might have been playing around, but you were checking things out, weren't you?'

Keith stubbed out his cigarette and pushed his fringe back from his creamy freckled face. He looked more boy than man, a sixth-former who was clever and worldly but still liked to kick cans up the road. He caught me looking at him and smiled before turning round to call for the bill. He stopped my arm reaching for my bag. 'Mr City's treat.'

'Thank you, Mr City.'

'Call me David,' he said. 'Please?'

We kissed goodbye out on the wet street, a soft kiss on the

65

lips, the smell of rain and engine oil in the air. It was cold, but Keith's breath was warm. The thrill of it took me by surprise.

'Yes, well,' I said, stepping back. 'I must go. Lovely lunch. Thanks.'

'Wait a minute,' he said, grasping my arm. 'I liked that, I want to do it again.'

So did I, and it didn't seem like a bad idea after so long, but I had made a promise to myself, to take more care.

'You've got work to do . . . and so have I.' I turned to walk briskly up Greek Street to the tube at Tottenham Court Road. Then I turned to see him still standing outside the restaurant, hands thrust in pockets, hair beginning to fall over his face. 'Give me a call, though, won't you?' I said.

He lifted his thumb up and waved, and so did I, before turning again to step lightly over the shiny puddles on the pavement. When I got to the station, I bought an *Evening Standard* and a copy of *Music Week* magazine. Any headline with Carla's name in it had me digging in my pocket for loose change nowadays.

The story I read was about Ghea's smooth distribution of Christmas product through one of the larger record companies which handled that side of the business for a number of independents. Dealers were said to be well pleased with the flow of singles, albums, tapes and CDs into their stores. Even with the unexpectedly high demand for "Seethru" and "The Unreleased Johnny Waits", the distribution companies had not suffered any delays or shortages from the factories.

'Well, thank heavens for that,' I said to myself, putting the magazine to one side and picking up the newspaper. I turned to Keith's page to discover where I should be living, eating, drinking and dancing or rather *seen* to be living, eating, drinking and dancing in London town. I'd reached the back page of the paper a few stations later and Stop Press carried a small item which I knew would be written up in depth for the last edition. It said:

Pirate who pre-launched Carla Blue's tapes found dead

66

in mysterious circumstances – Mr City.

I slumped back in the seat and stared at nothing. Keith was a quick worker, I had to hand it to him, and me? Me, I was losing my touch.

'You bastard!'

'Whatddya mean?' said Keith, all innocence.

'That was my story.'

'No, it wasn't. You hadn't made it at all. I made it. It was obvious.'

'But there is no connection.'

'The connection is what I said it was. Tommy Levi, a tape pirate, pre-launched two mega albums before the record company and is now dead. And his death was mysterious. I didn't say Ghea killed him. I don't even suggest it. I even have quotes from them saying that they informed the police, the BPI, the local trading standards offices. All I haven't got is St John saying the bastard deserved to die, but that would have been the cherry on the cake.'

He was right. It was the perfect story. The story that got people talking, got them asking 'What if?'

'George?' I remained silent. 'Look, George. Be honest. You weren't going to do anything with it, were you?' He waited patiently for my reply.

'Is that why you invited me to lunch? Mr City's treat for a tip.'

'I invited you before you told me, remember?' he replied firmly.

'I wasn't ringing in a tip.'

'OK. I won't pay you for the tip, if that makes you happier.'

'You creep! What about Tony Levi? It must have occurred to you that it's not in our interests to expose the counterfeiting story – he's not a pirate, by the way.' I added the last bit as a cheap shot, but it just made me sound more peeved.

Keith was quick to respond, and his answer made me feel

cheap and mercenary. 'Not in your interests, you mean.'

'You'll get something out of it. I told you,' I said, knowing that my answer wouldn't really compromise him.

'I don't really care, Georgina. You should know. Reporters often set up supposedly crooked deals in order to expose them, to prove what goes on. I thought that's what you would have been motivated by, not just to get a cheap shot at Ghea and St John for being too business-like about Carla's death, and certainly not to make money.'

His answer stung me. I hated him for exposing the story and exposing my motives in the cruel light of his own muted integrity. But, most of all, I hated myself. I had other problems, too. Tony Levi, for one. He wasn't going to like this at all. 'Thanks for everything, Keith. Let's hope you don't write about me next, because when Tony Levi gets to hear of this, my life won't be worth a sub's nut.'

'You sound more like your old self, Georgina. I'm sure you'll survive,' Keith replied breezily, and almost in the same breath added, 'By the way, when am I going to see you again?'

I put the telephone down and looked up. It was dark outside. The telephone rang again. I picked it up gingerly in the gloom of my front room.

'When?'

'Never!'

It had got dark already. I was too frightened to turn on the light for what might jump out at me from the early evening shadows. After two minutes that felt like ten, I did. Nothing was there. No ghosts. No Tony Levi. I paced up and down and thought about the things Keith and I had discussed. Then I picked up the phone, and dialled.

'David Richards.' It was his direct line.

I spoke as carefully and as menacingly as I could. 'Listen to me, you unbelievable shit. Don't get any ideas about running a story on Carla and me. If I get a whiff of it on your yuppie play page, I'll have your balls, that is if you've got any.'

'Hey, George . . . I really wouldn't have done that . . .'

The receiver was down before he could finish.

Chapter 6

It was only a matter of time. They'd put the numbers together and make four. I could just see St John chewing his dumb thumb, twitching in his office chair, and Dexter leaning back in his, listening to his PR man, watching him with those pale eyes. And Tony Levi? He'd be alone, standing by his hard wooden bar with the *Standard* neatly folded on it, drinking a small glass of cool beer. I was dead. Crushed. Oh yes. The Moving Finger writes; and having writ moves on: but I was left with everyone's damned finger pointed at me.

I looked at the telephone. Who'd be the first to call? Maybe they wouldn't. I looked at the door. Maybe they'd just drop by. Christ, he knew my address. Tony Levi paid the cab. He'd find out. He'd come and ask me to my face who told Mr City that Tommy sold counterfeit tapes, and who else knew. I'd blame Keith. I'd say I'd just been talking about our tape to Keith and happened to mention Tommy dying. Keith did it. He put the story together and I was the one who was getting squeezed. No one else knew. Only Keith. I hadn't told anybody. I sat in the dark, drinking and thinking. It wasn't my fault. It was Keith's. It was Keith's story. Some story.

The telephone rang, a persistent electronic warble, and I held my breath. It rang again. I let it go on for a little while before I got up, a little unsteadily, and reluctantly picked up the receiver.

'Georgina . . . the fuck you know about this story?'

'What story?' I said wearily.

'Keith – David – whatsisname Richards. Mr fucking City

just about saying Ghea fingered some street trader for selling tapes of Carla and Johnny Waits. Dexter's going up the wall. You seen it?'

'No.'

'The old Bill didn't pick up any of our tapes at Camden Lock – a load of other fucking junk, but no "Seethru", no "Unreleased". Now some dickhead called Tommy Levi's dead. You knew who was selling the tapes. How'd Mr City know, eh? I know he's a friend of yours, so don't give me any crap. You tell him? This Tommy Levi. You know him?'

'No.'

'This the guy you didn't tell me about on the plane?'

'It's possible, isn't it?'

'Listen, you better not be involved in this, know what I mean? You there? I said, are you there? What's goin' on? You pissed or what?'

Oh God, pressure, pressure, pressure . . . 'Not yet, but I'm trying very hard. Uh . . . must go, someone at the door. Thank you for your call.'

There really was. I dumped the receiver and St John's vulgar hysterical voice. The bell rang once, then twice, then three times. He knew I was in. I waited for a few more minutes. The knocking began. I placed my eye over the spyhole and he was looking right back at me through the fisheye, hands in suit pockets. Shit.

'Who is it?' I called feebly through the steel door.

'Tony.'

'Tony who?' I called again.

'Tony Levi.'

'Wait a minute.' I slid back the three steel bolts, unlocked the double security locks and unhooked the chain that could have kept him out. He stood outside until I stood back in the darkness and said 'Come in.'

'You had a power-cut or something?'

'No,' I fumbled around for a switch. 'I suffer from migraine.'

'Sorry to hear that,' he said, casting a quick glance around my untidy living-room. I began picking up the newspapers from the floor and my dressing-gown from the sofa. The wine bottle was emptying what remained of its contents on to the rug. I picked that up too and took it into the kitchen. The washing up was still in the sink.

Carla was laughing at me from somewhere in the back of my head. 'Why are you such a slob, George?' she said, dumping the cans in the bin.

'It's my very own dirty protest,' I said.

'Against what?' she asked flicking through my mail, one thigh on the side of my desk.

'The tyranny of oppressive neatness and conformity leading to the subjugation of all peoples who find it hard to find the right spot for a pair of knickers and tights after a tough night on the town. Can you make me a coffee, please?'

'Yes. But, jeez, it's a right mess.'

Oh, Carla, I'm in a right mess now.

'Coffee?'

'Yeah, why not? No milk, one sugar.'

'Why don't you sit down?' I called from the kitchen. I told myself he didn't matter. *Che serà, serà.* Let the wine do its trick. Cups, cups, where were the cups?

He knew I was drunk. I could see the frustration creeping over his hard face, as if he wanted to slap me around a bit to sober me up. He wanted to talk business, and I was unable to. He scared me, but he couldn't tell that. I was too relaxed, too loose about the edges for him to see fear.

'I'm sorry about your brother.'

He nodded and sat quietly drinking his coffee. He'd unbuttoned his jacket and was leaning forward in the chair, sipping from the mug, sharp elbows on knees, soft black leather lace-ups, neat black socks covering his slim ankles. His red paisley silk tie lay clipped to his white cotton shirt which was tucked into the trim waist of his trousers. Tony Levi kept himself in shape. He had broad straight shoulders, a narrow waist and, like his brother, was big boned for his height. His hands were wide across the knuckles, solid enough for the square ring. They'd make big fists. I could see him in a moody black and white photograph wearing baggy satin shorts and ankle boots, shoulders square, raised gloved hands on either side of his head, chin tucked in, and eyes looking steadily out from under those dark brows. Maybe that's how he got the dent on his nose and the crushed knuckle on his right hand. I didn't wait, I threw in the towel straight away.

'Look, about that piece in the paper, it wasn't right . . . '

'Yeah, well. They don't know nothing. The address wasn't important.'

What? Christ. He hadn't read the *Standard* yet. He was talking about the bit in the free-sheet. A message flashed up in my head like a warning beacon pulsating through the alcoholic haze. It was a reprieve. He placed his half-empty cup on the floor and made to stand up. 'Look, I thought you might be able to help me, but, excuse me, this is obviously not a good time.'

I looked across at him, trying hard to focus. I was saved. Now was the time to show him the door. But no, not me. Instead, I sat back for a moment, thoughtful and smug as a shrink, and then threw myself back into the fray. 'I'd like to help, if I can. I think I know how you feel . . . Well, almost. Carla was my best friend. She died last week, you know. She was my best friend,' I said, trying to check my own misery and give his time to breathe.

Tony looked at me blankly and then reached into the jacket of his dark suit, pulling out a photograph. It was a shot of a naked woman on a rumpled bed, slumbering in an adventurous postprandial pose. Even so, she looked familiar. 'You say you got friends in the music business. I think she's in the music business.'

'Why?'

'I found it with some other things.'

Uvver fings. It struck me then how childish the East London accent was. A two-year-old would say 'fing', not thing, 'fink', not think – words half grasped in an immature mind. But Tony Levi wasn't immature. This was a full-grown man in his mid-thirties, as smooth and savvy as any City broker who said thing, and think, and other. Perhaps, like the rest round here, once the words started working for him, he kept on using them and saved his wits for something else.

'You know her.' It wasn't a question.

'Well, yes, I know who she is,' I replied, trying to emphasise that she wasn't a friend, twisting the picture round and round to get a better look at her face.

'Who is she, then?'

'I think . . . Well, it looks like . . . I don't believe it! Yes, I think its Cheryl LeMat. Wife of Christian Dexter, you know, Ghea Records?'

No make-up, no fan-blown hair, no studio lights, no tapes on her breasts or ice-cubes on her nipples, no electrophotographic scanned removal of natural blemishes, no nothing – but it was her all right. Her betelnut-red hair streaming across the edge of the black satin bedsheets, her white wrists tied with a black belt. She looked happy to be trussed and tied, quite satisfied with the situation. 'It's not a typical shot of her,' I added, handing the photograph back.

He looked hard at it again, and shook his head. 'You're right. Yeah, you're right. Cheryl LeMat. Model, ain't she?'

'That what Tommy meant by class?'

He looked across at me, from under the brows. 'Yeah, well. You don't see much of that nowadays, do you?'

It stung, but only a little. My mind was elsewhere. I was thinking. Cheryl LeMat and Tommy. Dexter, LeMat and Tommy. There was a connection. Keith had made a connection, but not this one. Curiosity made me braver. I felt my head wobble a little as I asked the question, 'Why did you come here with that picture?'

He shrugged his shoulders. 'Tommy's dead. She might like to know.' He got up and shook his shoulders a little so that his jacket hung straight and buttoned up one button on the double-breasted front.

I got up, too, and walked over to the table by the telephone. Something inside kept telling me to show him the door, but I didn't listen, I showed him the *Evening Standard* instead.

It was difficult to tell, because the man's expression didn't change much, but he wasn't pleased. He unbuttoned his jacket again but didn't sit down. His eyes scanned the page and looked up at me once or twice. My mouth felt as if it were stuffed with cotton-wool. I stood about a yard from him, watching him slowly fold the paper over and over into a tight hard tube, and throw it. It winged past my ears like a baton and on to the sofa behind.

'You told some reporter that Tommy had those tapes? Yeah? Who else did you tell? Before you told that prick, before Tommy died?'

My heart was beating like the wings of a trapped bird. I was really frightened now. I didn't have a chance to explain that I hadn't told anyone. He wasn't in any mood to believe me. I stepped back, but he was stepping forward, rushing me, grabbing my shoulders and shaking me. My head rocked sickeningly back and forwards, back and forwards, on and on, until my stomach began to lurch and my throat tighten. I must have gulped convincingly because he pushed me away. I twisted dizzily round, pushing at him even though he wasn't there, and staggered waywardly towards the bathroom, locking the door. He didn't follow. I heard the front door slam, and sank to my knees.

An hour later, the telephone rang. It was Christian Dexter.

'Georgina, a word about this piece in the *Standard* . . .'

'I know. It wasn't my fault. Sorry, I can't talk right now.'

The mid-morning sun made no impression in the living-room where I had slept all night. No sound of birds, just the occasional footstep on a concrete floor and the grind of traffic in the road. My throat was as dry and sour as week-old bread. Tea. Fresh tea. Fresh leaf tea, I'd drink a scalding pot of it and die happy.

I deserved a worse headache than this. This one just felt like a tight band round my head. The worst ones are those that start off in the middle of your head, creaking like an old fishing-boat, and work out until you feel your skull is splitting apart like dry wood. I didn't feel sick either, just hungry. That was a good sign. If I could keep the tea down for ten minutes, then maybe I could eat something. Some toast and marmalade. I was still lying down, one leg hanging over the sofa, an arm crooked over my eyes.

Something, something: in headaches and in worry, vaguely life leaks away and Time will have his fancy, tomorrow or today. Carla liked that one. What was it called? She used to sit on the side of her desk reading out poems, her legs covered by long fawn socks and a heavy-duty pleated navy skirt. I could see the book, an anthology in a cover of abstract pink and black rectangles, but I couldn't hear her voice begin. Was she watching me now, looking down at me and shaking her head? I placed both feet gingerly on the navy carpet and stood up. Two, three, four. Not bad. Not bad at all. Oh no! The telephone. I'll kill whoever it is. I'll kill them! I'm not answering. I'm going into the kitchen. I can't stand the warble warble of it.

'Yes?' I gripped the receiver and leaned on the table.

'Georgina? Hi, it's me.' Keith's voice was hurried and businesslike.

'What?'

'I've got the sack.'

Silence.

'OK. OK. I know you're a bit pissed off with me, but hear me out. They sacked me over the Ghea story.'

Silence.

'They sacked me.'

'Probably, dear Keith, that's because a big fat writ hit the editor's desk within minutes of the paper hitting the stands. I'm not feeling very well right now, so I'm going to put the receiver down very, very quietly and make myself some tea. Don't call again.'

I looked around the room. Open some windows. Let some air in here. Then tidy up a bit. But nothing gets done until I get some tea. No, I didn't feel too bad.

Cheryl LeMat. I remembered while I was washing up. No cups for tea. They'd all called me. St John, Tony Levi, Dexter, Keith. I wondered what she had to say about all of this. Maybe I should talk to her, but would she talk to me? The suds billowed about in the bowl. It went: O plunge your hands in the water, plunge them in up to the wrist; stare stare in the basin, and wonder what you've missed. What was it? How did it begin again?

Those wet whirlpool eyes. Drugs. The connection was drugs. Tommy had died a snitch's death, a drug snitch's death. He sold them, and she looked as if she took them. She liked to get tied up, and he liked to take pictures. What if someone had found out? Someone who loved Cheryl LeMat? Dexter? Did he really love Cheryl LeMat like he'd loved Johnny Waits? Like he'd loved Carla? Dexter. Dexter. Dexter. Tea. Tea. Tea.

I was filling the kettle for the second time when the doorbell rang. I ignored it until whoever it was just leaned on the bell. I tiptoed towards the door and peeped through the spyhole. Keith. I went back to the kitchen, switched on the kettle and emptied the old tea into the sink. Keith started to yell.

'Go away!' I said through the door.

'Let me in, for just a minute?'

'Go away!'

'For fuck's sake, Georgina, open the bloody door!'

I replaced the chain – I'd been too preoccupied last night to lock up properly – then I slipped the latch. 'I don't know about your neighbourhood, but round here they don't hold with bad language,' I said through the crack.

Keith's pale face looked flushed, and he cast his eyes up to the ceiling as if a merciful God lodged in its stains. His collar was loose and his tie awry. I wanted to ask him why he'd bothered with the suit now that he could no longer start the day as Mr City. 'Oh yeah? Come on, ferchrissakes!'

'Have you brought any cigs?'

He patted his pockets in the old ritual and flashed a packet of B&H like a bus-pass. I didn't unhook the chain until he'd flicked it open and revealed at least fifteen in the pack.

'Welcome to my nightmare,' I said, as he stepped into the vortex of débris that was my living-room.

'Did I miss the party, or what? George, no one could accuse you of betraying the cause of feminism on the housework front.'

I ignored him and walked into the kitchen. He followed, and hung on the doorframe by one long arm as I poured myself some tea. I looked up, and he nodded enthusiastically. 'You've got a nerve,' I said, picking a clean mug off the draining-board and filling it with tea.

He pulled up a chair and sat opposite me at the kitchen table, offering me a cigarette and then sticking one in his mouth. He'd noticed the stack of bottles in a cardboard box by the plastic pedal-bin and looked hard at me as he steadied my hand while I lit up. 'You all right?'

I inhaled deeply, exhaled a plume of smoke into the sunlight and looked out of the window at the tower blocks.

'OK, listen to this and tell me what you think.'

I put my hand up like a policeman calling traffic to a halt. 'Just one minute, here. Just one minute,' I said. 'Do you realise the deep shit that you dropped me into yesterday? I got a call from just about every interested party, including a hands-on demonstration of deep dissatisfaction from one Tony Levi – who, by the way, thinks you are a prick and I am inclined to agree with him. And . . . wait a minute . . . and now you come beating my door down to run a few ideas past me? Do me a favour.'

Keith sat forward and spread both hands on the table like a magician showing the punters that he has nothing up his stuffed shirt-sleeves. His conscience had gone on permanent leave. 'OK, I apologise. Really, I'm sorry, but listen to this, please. It's very, very relevant.'

'Oh, get on with it.'

'Someone called yesterday to talk about the story. Well, you and I both know it was a wind-up, but I got a bite. Now this person was very distressed, to the point of being incoherent. What this person did manage to get across was that there was a connection between the Levi guy's death and Ghea. I couldn't get much else, not even a name, but I knew who it was. It was obvious. When I told them upstairs, I still got the boot.'

'So Ghea put pressure on, so what? Who was the distressed person?' I said, feeling a strong groundswell of precognition.

'Guess.'

I took a sip of tea, a puff of my cigarette, flicked some ash and exhaled two smoke-rings that hovered between us and then melted away. 'Cheryl LeMat?'

Keith's goldfish expression confirmed it. I pushed the green glass souvenir of the Lake District towards his hand so that the leaning tower of·ash at the end of his cigarette would fall into it, and got up wearily for a tea refill.

'You're right, of course. She was crying, so I didn't get much, but she kept saying over and over that they had killed Tommy. Over and over.'

I waited until he had ground his cigarette out, then I ʝicked up the ashtray and walked into the living-room. I sat ʼn the sofa and looked around, only slightly aware of a ꞇeadache that asserted itself every time I moved up or down a level. They were right. The place was a mess. It was about time I got myself straight. The vacuum cleaner was in a cupboard by the bathroom. No harm in seeing if it still worked.

The sound brought Keith to the doorframe. I was pushing the brush across the carpet and picking up old newspapers, magazines and Kentucky Fried Chicken cartons on my way around the room. After a couple of minutes, he walked behind me and dragged the plug from the wall.

'So what have you got?' he said.

I sat down again on the sofa, and he came and sat

opposite, in the chair that Tony Levi had occupied the night before. There was nothing intimidating about Keith, even if he was a little pissed off. He sat back in stylish disarray, scraping his hair back from his face, exuding that mix of worldliness and naïve cunning that is so common in the university educated; particularly if they have lived in a squat for a few months and had a couple of jobs which paid cash in hand. But to compare him with Tony Levi would be to compare a house-trained Dalmatian to a tree-living leopard. I didn't answer him.

'Anyone call you?' he said, trying a more indirect approach.

'I told you, everyone called me.'

He leaned forward and pressed his fingers together. 'Look, George, I tell you that someone calls me to tell me that there is a connection between Tommy Levi's death and Ghea, and you guess right first time. Now, come on, give a little! We could be onto a big story here!'

'Keith, if you have a story, then be my guest and go for it. Now, excuse me.'

The sound of persistent vacuuming filled the flat again, and Keith hung around until he realised that, despite all contrary indications, I really was quite houseproud. After he'd left, I carried a large plastic bag full of rubbish to the chute to the end of the hall outside and dropped it down. As I opened the hatch, the sweet sickly smell of decomposition rose into my nostrils and set me scuttling back to the flat, clutching my throat. I cleaned the bathroom again and made myself some more tea.

Cheryl LeMat. A £10,000-a-day beauty, married to one of the most prominent men in the music business, crying down the phone to Mr City over a street trader who dabbled in more than one illegal commodity. Interesting. Keith, bless him, had brought me an important corner piece of a new puzzle. I remembered the things that Tony Levi had said the night before, and the picture. Drink didn't make me forgetful. On the contrary, I could always remember the details, especially the ones I wanted to forget. But why should Ghea – and for Ghea read Christian Dexter – want Tommy Levi out of the way? Surely not for the tapes. Maybe for the picture of Cheryl LeMat? I'd buy that, and so would Tony Levi, which was why he wanted to see her.

Chapter 7

The bar was empty and about to close when I arrived. The barmaid was loading up a tray of glasses for the glasswasher. Tony obviously didn't do afters.

''Allo, luv,' she said with a big lipsticky smile. Her large pneumatic breasts were imprisoned in a white shawl blouse and decorated with at least three gold chains of varying thicknesses, from one of which hung the letter T.

'Is Tony about?'

'Who shall I say?'

'Georgina . . . Powers.'

She picked up the telephone, still watching me while she spoke. Then she smiled again and nodded. 'Round here, luv.'

She opened a door behind the bar and pointed along a long corridor lined with cardboard boxes of flavoured crisps and plastic crates of beer and mixers. The stairs at the end were badly lit and the carpets smelled of damp and age. When I got to the first floor landing, I heard a dog snuffling and snarling under the bright gap of a door. I knocked. Then the barking began. It now sounded like two dogs, two big deep-throated dogs. A man's severe voice silenced them, and then the door opened. I stayed where I was.

'Come in.' Tony Levi tilted his head into the room, but didn't smile. I still didn't move, so he opened the door wide. 'Come in. Come on. They won't touch you.'

'Yes, but can we say the same about you?' I said, as I stepped into the gloomy room. He didn't reply; he just carried on walking away from me.

Tony Levi's two large, square-headed, brown and black Rottweilers lay side by side by a big black leather armchair. They looked disappointed, with their huge saliva-flecked jaws propped disconsolately on their stubby paws, their meaty brows wrinkled in reproachful furrows. No animal psychologist required here. These boys knew their place. That must be the secret of a good untroubled life. Rules, consistency and security. Everyone knew what was expected of him and what to expect if he stepped out of line.

'Sit over here,' Tony said, pointing away from the armchair to a large sofa that appeared to have a kingsize black leather duvet cast over it.

I sat down on it and crossed my legs, first one way and then the other. 'I like dogs, actually. I used to have one.'

He walked away from me again, this time up a couple of steps to a breakfast bar that separated a galley kitchen from the dining area. 'Suppose that helps,' he said.

It had been two large rooms before the architects and interior designers had moved in. Some remnants of Victoriana remained; the coving and cornices, the sash windows. The rest of the place looked less than three years old. The fireplace was a modern cubic recess half-way up one wall, glowing warmly with the homely light of heat-resistant black ceramic coals and blue gas-flames. The patterned carpet was deep red, Persian style; the dining-room suite, black laquered, Italian style; the kitchen smoothly lined with the finest grey laminate, probably German; all appliances also German, black, flush and integral. The stereophonic sound system was too far away for me to see in detail, but it had to be Danish-style Bang and Olufsen. It sat darkly and discreetly on the glass and brass shelves that also bore a record collection of considerable proportions. There were some black-framed pictures on the white walls, mainly pugilistic portraits, charcoal sketches and watercolours of turn-of-the-century bouts and a white plaster simulacrum of a youthful, straight-nosed, Ancient Greek athlete stood awkwardly in one corner, hand outstretched as if someone was about to pass him his clothes. Apart from these items, and the leather suite, the room was bare. There was no clutter and there were no curtains, just fine grey Venetian blinds tilted so that the dim light of the afternoon sun hardly penetrated.

Tony raised a large green bottle of Gordon's with the label on upside-down. 'Drink?'

I shook my head. The dogs sighed, and Tony stepped into his kitchen and filled his coffee-filtering machine. When he returned, he sat in the chair by his dogs. 'What you got for me, then?' The coffee machine spluttered and hissed while he put his hands together and cracked his knuckles.

'I came to see if we still had a deal.'

'Why not?'

'Oh, silly me. I didn't realise that a good shaking was an old East End business custom.'

'It is when one party crosses the other.'

'Well, since that is not the case, how about an apology?'

He gave his knuckles a rest and started rubbing his index finger round the soft neck of his black and cream Argyll cashmere. 'What for? For dropping Tommy in it? And me?'

'I didn't.'

'Well, seems to me, Tommy's troubles began the day he met you . . . What with all your friends in the music business.'

'I think they began before that.'

His mouth was pursed tight and pulled downwards, the way men looked when they wanted to control some emotion or other, anger, bitterness – sadness, sometimes. Tony's hazel eyes didn't look sad. They looked as dark and unreal as his black ceramic coals. He started to drag the index finger and thumb of his right hand down his left trouser-leg, sharpening its pure wool crease. He grinned a little while his hand went slowly up and down. 'A misunderstanding, then?'

'I think there was. I think you lost your cool.'

He stopped grinning. 'I think I lost a brother.' There it

was again, that juvenile way of speaking – fink instead of think and bruvver instead of brother. But his accent was nothing to coo over, it was unemotional and menacing.

'It wasn't my fault.'

'Tell me about it.'

It was pure method acting. He uncrossed his legs and sat staring at me steadily and squarely like Pacino as Don Michael Corleone in *Godfather II* or was it *III*? The bit at his mother's funeral when he listens patiently while his sister pleads forgiveness for fumbling brother Fredo. He pats her hand, squeezes her cheek and then gives Fredo the fool a big brotherly hug in front of the family. The poor sap gets blown to so much fishbait on his next angling trip on the lake. If I had just met Tony, and there was nothing between us, I would have pointed this out to him, provided I'd had a few drinks. Asked him if he'd seen the film, practised the part. Right now, I didn't think he would appreciate the comparison. His sense of humour was as vestigial as a snake's leg.

'David Richards – I still call him Keith from the days when he played with Carla Blue's back-up band – was Mr City. He's on the tape I gave you, playing the sax and the guitar. Yesterday, the day I read about Tommy's death, I told Keith about our deal – I thought there might be a problem. In passing, I told him that Tommy was the guy I'd bought the "Seethru" and "The Unreleased Johnny Waits" from, prior to their launch. He thought it was pretty funny. But, like the good friend he is, he put two and two together and made five, thus dipping me right in it. Then he lost his job. Ghea were a little upset with the paper. You see, he made up the connection. It was just a story.'

Tony didn't say anything. He sat back, flexing his hands, his two gold rings glinting a little in the poor light. The dogs were asleep – well, their eyes were closed – so I thought I'd push my luck. 'So what's it to be? Fishbait or an apology?'

His eyebrows peaked over his nose and a slight flicker of confusion registered in his eyes. Now he really looked like Tommy. 'You what?'

'An apology?'

He shrugged, and rested his clean manicured hands flat on the leather armrests of his chair. He took his time. 'OK. I shouldn't have gone for you like that. I was well out of order.'

I raised my eyebrows in encouragement, but he ignored me. It was the best that I could expect. The coffee machine signalled its final splutter, so he got up and walked up the steps towards the kitchen.

'You're a journalist. Computers, eh? What you getting out of this?'

Trouble, I said to myself as he picked up the internal telephone and spoke to the barmaid downstairs. His black portable telephone lay together with his black personal organiser/calculator on the square brass and glass table that had separated us.

'OK, Trace, I'll be down,' he said, and replaced the receiver. Then he went into the kitchen to pour the coffee, which he delivered to the table on a black laquered platter set with white porcelain cups on delicate saucers, and an elegant little milk-jug and sugar-bowl to match. I tried to remember whether I'd given him his coffee in a British Telecom standard issue mug or one that bore the logo 'I think therefore IBM'.

'Well?' he said, straightening up.

'It was an old business card. I haven't worked in a while.'

He didn't comment. He just indicated the coffee and walked out of the room – down towards the bar, I presumed. I spooned a teaspoon of sugar into the cup, and stirred the liquid with a little silver spoon. I checked out the dogs. Their eyes were open and fixed upon me, so I sat very still until Tony came back carrying the till drawers. He put them down on the dining-room table and then came and sat in the armchair again. The dogs rolled over and closed their eyes, while I set my empty cup and saucer down on the table with a bell-like rattle.

'I do have some questions, though.'

'I asked what you had for me. You still haven't answered.'

My move again. If I told him, he'd have no need to tell me

anything. If I didn't, I'd have to force the answers out of him. That would be as easy to achieve as a rebate from the taxman. 'Keith had a call from Cheryl LeMat. She was very upset. She told him that there was a connection between Tommy's death and Ghea.'

Now Tony put his cup and saucer down on the table and looked away. His jaw was clenched tight enough to show a little muscle twitch on the side of his face. My future felt as secure as poor brother Fredo's, but it didn't stop me from pleading.

'Look, I told you. I didn't say anything about Tommy until after he was dead. He died on Sunday, didn't he? Believe me, I spoke to Keith on Thursday. He wrote the story on Thursday. He didn't know anything about the tapes or Tommy until then.'

Tony raised a hand to reassure me, so I let him be for a couple of minutes. Then I asked my questions. 'You said a couple of things last night. You said you found the photographs *with other things*, and you asked me who I had told *before* I told Keith. What's on your mind?'

Tony looked back at me. His eyes narrowed slightly, but other than that he registered neither surprise nor curiosity. 'I found the photograph in Tommy's slaughter . . . '

I raised a curious eyebrow.

' . . . His stash . . . He was a tealeaf – thief – you know, among other things, and he had lots of gear in there: dope, tapes and the dirty photos. Whoever killed him wanted some or all of it. If someone had fingered him for the tapes, it could've been you. You asked questions in the pub.'

'Who'd I tell?' I said.

No answer.

'I suppose Tommy wouldn't tell, and that's why they killed him?'

'You suppose wrong. He told them all right. Whoever it was cleared him out, the lot.'

I waited and he waited. He knew what I was going to have to ask, and for a moment I thought I saw danger, the brief glint in his gloating eyes. I thought, just for a moment, that I'd walked right into a trap. 'How come you found the slaughter, Tony? And got that photograph?' I said. I was as close to praying as I'd been since my first missed period. It was possible that he would spring the 'for it was I' routine on me and then wake his dogs up for supper. I was stuck there with all the mobility of a bag of dog-bones.

'Insurance. I always knew where Tommy kept his gear. I always kept a record of what Tommy was up to, just in case.'

I reached into my bag for one of Keith's B&Hs. Relief had not brought relaxation. 'Do you mind if I smoke?' I said.

'Yeah.'

The perfect host. I shrugged, a little embarrassed, and replaced the packet in my bag, clicking it shut. Now what? I nodded at the pictures. 'Yes, you seem to keep pretty fit . . . Er, are you in the boxing game?'

'Was. Could've been a contender and all that.'

I smiled. Well, I couldn't let it go. It was his first little joke of the day. But I carried on looking around his flat so that I didn't have to look at him. What would Carla have made of him? What indeed.

There are two types of men, she used to say; men who like women and men who don't like them at all; but you've got to watch out for both, because it's damned difficult to tell for sure which is which. In any case, she concluded, both types can be a real pain and are no real advantage to women at all. Now, which pain was Tony? I'd say he didn't like women, with the proviso that I only had my own experience with him to go on, and the circumstances were unusually negative, to say the least. Even so, he lacked gentleness. You could see that in everything he did. He was cruel. Maybe he just didn't like anyone. What about sex? He was handsome, all right, but that never was enough. I could imagine him naked, shining with the unnatural pallor that distinguishes a white fighter, but alone. He'd be like the white plaster Olympian in the corner, only with a dent in his noble nose. No, I couldn't imagine Tony with a woman, but I could imagine him leaving. He'd be shutting the door on someone in a rumpled bed, in a room that wasn't his own, fully dressed and leaving, without looking back.

Now Tommy, he definitely liked women. I could see him with any number of women, laughing, rumpled, flushed and sweaty, lighting two cigarettes, squeezing breasts and buttocks, sending flowers. A ladies' man. Or was he? He wasn't the faithful sort. He played around. He didn't make it easy or safe for a woman to be with him. And what about those photographs? She looked happy all right, but why did he take them? Maybe he didn't like women, after all. Maybe he just pleased himself, messed them up and didn't care. Like the girl said, damned difficult to tell.

'Do you live here?' I said.

'When I'm in town, yeah. It's an office really.' He stood up and stuck his hands in his pockets. End of interview. One of the dogs yawned and slapped its chops together. I picked up my bag, wondering if, before I got out of the door, I could bring myself to ask him whom he thought had killed Tommy.

'What's your interest in all this?' he said, taking the decision-making right out of my hands.

I was desperate for a cigarette now. What was my interest? In dead junkies and pirate tapes, Mrs Dexter's infidelities? I didn't really know. I only half knew until then. Since Carla's death, I'd been in a dream-like fog just feeling my way around. Tommy's death had started to burn it away, leaving little rocks of intuition peeking through a thinning mist. I hadn't come to any conclusion before now, and now was as good a time as any to test it.

'Well, I think . . . I think . . . whoever killed your Tommy may . . . have killed Carla Blue, my friend Carla. But I don't know why.'

Tony's hazel eyes were a little more generous now, a little more alive. 'Well, Georgina, I, for one, think you're dead right.'

Coming to terms with Carla's death was one thing. I

hadn't managed that yet. But coming to terms with her murder was quite another. The desultory knowledge within me had finally surfaced and I had had no time to deny it, ease myself into the truth. He hadn't called me a fool or even shrunk from the horror of it. He had confirmed it. In his world, murder was a possibility, a probability. In my world, it was unexpected. I couldn't speak for a long while, and he didn't try. There was silence until the winter sun finally withdrew its light from the room and Tony switched on a side light.

'Do you need a drink?' Not want, need.

I nodded. He gave me a Scotch. Scotch for shock. Gin for sin. I took a long swallow with my eyes closed. I didn't care if he saw it, but I wanted him to see that I handled it. He'd judge me by what he saw, and I'd judge him by what he said about it. But he didn't say anything. The spirit burned my lips and the frenzied action in my mind slowed up to an acceptable level. The relief of it made me want to cry. 'Any ideas?' I said, putting down the empty glass, but still holding it in my hand.

'You met this Cheryl LeMat?'

I looked up. I ask a question, he answers with a question. 'At a Ghea party last Saturday. She was with her husband, a bit tense,' I said.

'You think Dexter did it?'

'He could have done. Look, I know you know. You've got something. Why are you asking me?'

He spun the black metallic top on the Scotch and topped both glasses up. 'OK. I've got the stuff Tommy had. You haven't. So what makes you think the same person killed your mate?'

'A few things. One, he was with her when she died, down by the pool. Two, she had taken a lot of heroin, but as far as I knew, she'd never tried the stuff. Three, he was with Johnny Waits when he died of a heroin overdose. What if he helped him on his way? If he did, then he knows how to get away with something like that.'

'Motive?'

'I don't know. Money, possibly. Alive or dead, she was worth a fortune. Jealousy. I don't know. Dammit, I don't know. All I know is that no one seemed to care when she died, not her manager John St John, not Dexter – they were pleased, if anything, pleased with the way her albums were selling . . . Look, I've got to have a cigarette.'

I tugged at my bag, and lit up regardless. Tony shifted the saucer from under his coffee-cup and pushed it towards me. I felt guilty, but he didn't seem bothered now.

'What about this St John bloke?'

'Yes. He could kill someone. He'd do it onstage if it would pull a crowd. But I can't think of a reason why he'd want to kill Carla, not really.'

'So why do you think Dexter wanted to kill her?'

'He had some sort of relationship with her. Maybe it's something to do with that.' I took a deep drag of the cigarette and exhaled away from him. He was still listening, but I'd finished.

'You don't like that,' he said.

'What?'

'Her with him.'

My face warmed a little with irritation as much as embarrassment. Either it showed, or Tony was more sensitive than I'd given him credit for. I ignored his question and got back to the drugs. 'She was sniffing cocaine at the party. I know she did that. But heroin's different. I don't think she did that stuff.'

'Look. I read the papers, morphine in the system means heroin. It's a fact. You can OD taking too much smack or smack that's too pure. And you don't have to be a junkie to OD. It's all down to tolerance. If you got no tolerance, that's it. It can take an hour or half a day, but your skin goes blue, your pupils go like pissholes in the snow, you can't breathe properly, then you go into a coma and die because your lungs and heart choke up. Look, junkies OD after they've been in the nick or in hospital for a while and haven't been using. They get out and shoot up at the old strength, or shoot up a dose that ain't 95 per cent baby laxative, or they take all they've got if they don't know if they're gonna get any more. An addict's daily half a g. will kill someone with no tolerance. 'Course, if you drink as well, you can die just choking on your own puke.'

'You seem to know a lot about it.'

He didn't answer that. 'Look, toot speeds you up, but you really got to go some to OD on it. Some people mix it with smack or methadone and inject it. She didn't do that, did she? Did they find any holes in her? In her arms, in her legs, up her fanny?'

'I don't know. What if she sniffed heroin, thinking it was cocaine?'

'There you go.'

God, it was so easy. He poured me some more Scotch. Anyone could have given her the stuff to sniff. How experienced was she to know the difference? But someone had to make sure she went down to the pool as well. 'They didn't kill Tommy for the tapes, did they?' I said, drinking a little more.

'Nah, don't think so. The tapes were the homing device, know what I mean? They wanted those photographs – the one I took was the only one that showed her face.'

'What about the dope?'

'They took the dope.'

'So who . . . You think Dexter?'

'Got to be.'

'Do we call the police?'

'What do you think?'

I flicked some ash into the white coffee-ringed saucer. Now that we were a team, I could tell him. 'Listen. Let's get one thing straight. *I*'m the journalist; *I* get to ask the questions.'

There it was, that scary elusive smile. 'Yeah, well, us villains, we don't like to answer other people's questions. It means they already half know the answers, know what I mean?'

I smiled too, and nodded. 'All right. But do we tell the police?'

'Tell them what? Tell them all about our tape business?'

My glass was empty. He showed me the bottle, but I shook my head. I was at just the right stage for thinking. The next stage would be just right for having a good time. After that, nothing would go right.

'I got something to show you,' he said, getting up and making his way towards a door that I presumed led to the rest of his flat. 'Computer stuff. You know about computers, doncha?'

No one who knew anything about computers said that. People who worked around computers liked buzzwords. They knew the jargon. They said machine, kit, disks, floppies, printout.

'I'm a bit out of touch,' I called to his disappearing back.

'I don't fuckin' believe it.'

Tony had not sworn before, so I reckoned this was bad news. He'd returned with a sheaf of papers, pushed the cups and glasses aside and spread the blank pages out on the coffee-table. The dogs were awake now and seemed to be looking at me like it was my fault. They made me nervous.

'What's up?' I said.

'Someone's been and swapped the stuff I copied with this lot. There's nothing here.'

'It's supposed to be a copy of a computer printout?'

'Yeah. Yeah.' He was thinking now, impatient with my prattle.

'Who, then?'

'Oh Christ! Who? I don't fucking know, do I?'

He bounced up from the chair and swiped the paper off the table with such force that the delicate white cups scattered and smashed and our glasses tumbled onto the floor. The dogs rose growling as Tony walked away from us. I sat immobilised by the uncertainty of the situation. Then he turned round and gripped the back of his chair, hanging his head between his straight, muscular arms. After a

couple of minutes he looked up, and pushed himself upright.
'Tommy. Got to be,' he said, calmer now.

'Tommy?'

'Tommy. The stupid effing git. He'd been in and taken the lot.'

Ah, Tommy. I had to admire him, taking it upon himself to face the two-headed Cerberus just to protect his privacy. It seemed that big brother Tony wasn't the only one who liked to take insurance. There was a funny side to this, but now was not the time to put it to Tony. I spoke gently to him, trying to sound helpful. 'Do you remember what it was about?' I said.

'Yeah, not all, but I got the general idea.'

'What was it?'

'A computer-generated report. Financial report, sort of.'

'Ghea's?'

'Yeah.'

'How'd Tommy get it?'

'From her gaff, same time he got the tapes.'

'Must have been important, then. Did you read it through?'

'Leave it, will you?'

His jaw clamped tight and his lips moved over his teeth like there was a stringy piece of meat stuck in them. One of the dogs gave a little whine and sat back on its haunches, gazing at Tony like a concerned parent at a troubled child. He walked around the front of the chair and sat down, legs apart, leaning forward with his arms resting lightly on his knees. He spoke in brisk, shamefaced tones that a young man reserves for the time when he has to tell his girl that she might have an unspecified sexually transmitted disease, and that she might have caught it from him.

'I've got a problem, and you might have, if they think you got a connection here. The copies were done on my machine, on the pub paper. I was doing it quick, and I didn't change the cassette. If Tommy took them, he's either slung them or put them back in his slaughter. If he put them back with the originals, whoever did him has got the lot, and has got to know that I've seen them. He's got the tapes, too – "Seethru", "The Unreleased Johnny Waits" and the one you gave me. Let's hope he don't know nothing about our deal, because then he'll start thinking about how much you know.'

I had to think about what he'd said. Keith. He was the only one who knew about the deal, and he was proving to be most unreliable. 'Look, he may not necessarily make those connections. Anyway I thought you said the killer wanted the photographs.'

'Yeah, well . . . C'mon, I'll take you home.'

I stood on the busy corner by the traffic lights waiting for Tony to bring his car round the front. I knew what car he would be driving before I saw it pull up. It was only a question of what size and what colour. He would have to pick a straight down-the-line-class motor with no gaudy accessories. There it was. A sleek grey shark-faced BMW 525i, the Gucci loafer of the road. But ultimate driving machine or no, I didn't like the way Tony handled it. Anger affected his performance. We jerked too fast up to red lights and sped between lanes on the busy Mile End Road towards Bow until I began to feel my hangover had really only taken a short afternoon break. He was annoyed about the report, but I bet he was none too pleased about having to admit a mistake to me either.

'Look, let me out. I can get a cab,' I said, gripping the armrest.

He looked in the mirror, changed gear, pulled out to overtake the cab I'd had my eye on, and put his foot down. My head pressed against the back of the seat. 'I said I'd see you home. I want to check you get in all right and lock yourself in.'

'You're a very calming influence on me, did I ever tell you that? What about the pub?'

'Trace'll open up.'

We didn't say any more until he swung the car into a space

94

in the parking lot at the foot of my block. We both got out, and he locked the car.

'Look, you can't leave that here. I'll be all right,' I said, but he just walked around to my side and put a firm hand on my elbow.

'It's insured. Now come on.'

Tony walked on briskly without another word and led me upstairs. Then he made me wait by the open door of my flat while he went around switching on all the lights. For a change, the place didn't look as if Hurricane Hugo had swept through it. As a rule, I couldn't care less how it was or who saw it, but just tonight I liked the order of it and I liked not seeing someone screw up their nose when they walked in. A little red light flashed on and off on my answering machine. I walked over, rewound the tape and pressed 'play'.

'Beep. Hi, this is Dav . . . Keith. Bet you're missing me. Look, I tried to set up an interview with Cheryl LeMat. No go. There's something in this. Call me.'

'Beep. It's St John. Dexter tells me you got a tape that we could be interested in. Better call me.'

'Beep. This is Christian Dexter. 5.00 p.m. Friday 8th December. I believe you have an early tape of Carla Blue. Do not attempt to distribute it. Please call Ghea on Haslemere 2879 after 7.30 p.m.'

Tony stood with his arms folded in the middle of the room, and I opened my bag to dig out a cigarette. It was time to think. I was glad I'd told Tony about Cheryl LeMat now that he'd heard Keith's message. But Keith must have told Dexter and St John about the tape, and I couldn't understand why. What was he playing at?

'This Dexter's going to make a sure-fire connection now, ain't he?' said Tony.

I threw my bag on a chair and walked across to the sofa to sit down. For once, Tony was following me about, explaining.

'One. He's got the report back and the copies with my

name on 'em, and he's got the photographs of the wife. Two. He's got the tapes. Finds out one of them's your tape, from that prick Keith, knows you're getting it copied and by whom. Three. He now knows we know. You don't need an O level to work that out.'

I blew smoke out across the room. Tony was still standing up with his arms folded. He was looking at me, wondering why I hadn't said anything. Perhaps he thought I was afraid, but I was tired. I was tired of keeping watch. There was no one around to trust. Not Keith. Not St John. Not Dexter. And Tony? He'd played me like a fish to see if I would bite. I'd come to the conclusion he'd known all along. He'd known something about Carla's death because he had seen that report. Now that he didn't have it, he was worried that someone knew he'd seen it. Tommy's killer. Dexter. So now what?

'He knows we might know something, that's all. What's the problem, Tony? What was on that printout?'

'Statistics'.

'Go on.'

'Sales forecasting. Confidential stuff.'

'Go on.'

'It was stuff on the business. It laid out a whole load of stuff: advertising spend, market sector, singles success in a year, albums success in a year, regional and international variations, concerts in a year, tours, amount of editorial coverage, negative, and positive – and showed how all that affected sales. Like I said, a whole load of stuff.'

'So far, so boring,' I said.

'Right.'

'So why are we standing here with all the lights switched on?'

No answer.

'Did you know that Ghea was going public? Dexter stands to make a fortune.'

'No, I didn't know that,' he said, looking down at his sleek gold watch. 'I got to go. You going to call him?'

96

I leaned forward and ground out my cigarette. 'Wait a minute. Tell me what's going on.'

'I dunno.'

'I don't believe you.' The look he gave me said what I thought didn't matter this much. Even so, I wasn't about to give up. 'Look, with all due respect, Tommy didn't strike me as the sort who knew his way around a financial report. Why'd he take it?'

Tony was already walking towards the door.

'Maybe he was given it. Know what I mean?' he said, turning the handle and walking out.

'Tony!'

I didn't say goodbye as he shut the door. Damn the man. Cheryl LeMat knew. Had she given Tommy the report to get at her own husband? I wanted to talk to her now, and I hoped Keith hadn't scared her off already with his fast flip-over spiral-ringed scoop reporter's notebook. I wondered about calling Dexter about the tape, but I changed my mind. I didn't want to start asking him questions yet, so I called St John instead. Might as well get it out of the way.

'You got a fucking nerve, you know that?' St John had no in-between stage. When he hit the wall, he hit it like a cannon of water from a fireman's hose.

'Look, Carla gave me the tape. I wanted to do something with it,' I said.

'Why didn't you come to me? I'm her agent, remember?'

'Well, I just got talking to this guy and he made me an interesting offer.'

'The dead bloke. This Tommy Levi?'

'Yes, as it happens . . . Look, what's the big deal? I don't know why Keith bothered you all with it. It's not as if Ghea had anything to do with the tape in the first place.'

'What's the big deal? What do you know? Nothing. Number one, Carla's my client. Everything she did has something to do with me. Number two. Keith and Mick have made a deal with Ghea. So I got a lot to do with it. Ghea has a lot to do with it.'

'Oh.'

'Yeah. Oh. Now we don't want a deadshit pirate selling it before we do.'

'Like before?' This brought him up short. He didn't come back with a fast answer. I saw an opportunity to push home a point. 'Well, he won't be. Don't worry. He's dead, isn't he? One thing, though; did you ever find out how Tommy got those tapes?' I said.

'No. Did you?' St John's voice was lower and quieter now.

'No.'

'Why?' he said cautiously.

'I heard a whisper that the lovely Mrs Dexter was seen around with this guy Tommy.'

'That right?'

'Yeah. Just a whisper. Might have been her. C'mon, St John, you must know. Is that why Ghea got so nervous about Keith's story?'

'Fucking journalists! Where'd you get this stuff?'

'Aw, come on, St John. Is Dexter the jealous type?'

'Look, that story came out of Keith's stupid turnip head. What does Ghea know about some junkie dying in the East End? Why would Cheryl LeMat knock around with that sort of low life? She's beautiful. She's got class.'

'I don't know, St John. I was hoping you'd tell me.'

'Forget it. Just keep out of trouble, all right? And get that fucking tape back.'

'What if it's too late?'

'Then you are in deep shit.'

'Thanks, St John,' I said, and put the receiver down. After that, I didn't want to speak to Keith or Dexter, but I tried Dexter anyway. The phone was engaged.

Chapter 8

Heavy rain whipped across my bedroom window in wind-driven waves. Fifteen shopping days to Christmas, the man said, and then played me a jingle that sounded like fifteen Morris men in a bag. There was something else. The telephone was ringing.

'It's me. Are you in bed?' Keith's voice was bright and urgent.

'I am going to kill you, Keith,' I said, my eyes tightly closed, my head buzzing just a little under the dark cover of the duvet.

'Sorry. I wanted to catch you before you went out.'

'Went out where?'

'Shopping.'

'Keith, I am going to kill you.'

'C'mon George, don't be like that . . . I want to talk to you about the tape.'

I stretched out my arm from the warmth of my crumpled duvet bivouac, dropped the receiver with a clatter and slept for another hour and a half.

It was still raining as I ate breakfast. Steam rose in hot wisps from the spout of the kettle and began to fog the cold windowpane. It was warm in the kitchen, but the rain against the glass made me shiver. I popped the last piece of toast and marmalade into my mouth and stared down at crumbs and sticky blobs of orange on my empty plate. There was half a pizza and a quarter of strong Cheddar in the fridge, a catering portion of salad cream that had been there far too long, some beers and a quarter of a bottle of white wine. It was not appropriate, and it was not enough. My stomach yearned for eggs, bacon, sausages, tomatoes and maybe even some black pudding and brown sauce. Fried, with soft quarters of white bread edged with hard seeded crusts to dip into the dark yellow yolks, pork fat and tomato juice. Shopping. In the rain. Walking home with lumpy plastic carrier bags and my feet all wet. I shut the fridge door and looked at my watch. 11.00 a.m. Maybe I could go to a café for a fry-up and get some stuff on the way home. The telephone rang on my way out of the front door.

'Hi.'

'Keith, I'm going out.'

'Shopping? In this rain? Glad I caught you. About tonight. We're going to Wiggy's.'

'Keith, I don't ever want to see or hear from you again.'

'Look, I can explain about the tape. It's part of the plan.'

'Plan?'

'Yes. We're working together on this story, whether you like it or not. Meet me at Polo's first, we'll eat about nine, and then we can go on to Wiggy's.'

'Keith, I do not have a Gaultier jacket and I'm not paying a tenner a round. Tell me the plan now.'

'Look, there's a fashion agent's birthday thrash there tonight. I can guarantee Cheryl LeMat won't miss it,' he said.

Now I *was* tempted, even with Keith for company and at those bar prices. 'OK. See you at nine,' I said.

'Great!'

'Goodbye, Keith.'

I went out and got my breakfast. It was easy to think in the packed café. A sales report. What could be worth killing for in that? Unless the sales were extraordinarily good, or bad. It was interesting, but so what? I looked down at my white oval plate, wiped clean of any trace of yolk, juice and sauce. There was just a greasy film on its surface and I could hardly believe that anything had lain there. I'd been in the café half an hour and it seemed like five minutes.

*

'What do you want?' said Keith, looking around, rainwater dripping off his fringe onto the shiny brass bar.

'A marguerita. Lots of crushed ice.'

The black barman wearing a sharp white shirt and black waistcoat pushed our drinks silently towards us and left the tab in a glass. The smart piano bar was crowded with an entire cast of bright young things taking a breather from the party downstairs. The wide staircase repeated the gilt and drape rococo theme of the bar to where the sleek stylish dancers thrashed about in a large wooden corral. The crowded dancefloor was surrounded by little medieval balconies furnished with marble-topped tables and leathery benches, and the sound was orchestrated by a fast-fingered jock ensconced above the floor in a little green-curtained box. Keith and I moved around peering into this panorama of kinetic art for the red-haired Cheryl LeMat, our shoes damp and sodden. It was as steamy as a tropical rainforest in there, yet black-bereted black guys in velvet-collared Crombies stood around with their trousers tucked into shiny Doc Marten boots. Beautiful women with white faces and crimson lips draped themselves against them like yawning leopards. But Cheryl LeMat wasn't one of them.

An hour later we were back at the bar, and Keith mopped his damp head with a bar towel and sighed with frustration. He looked even younger than usual with strips of dark wet hair curling over his wide freckled forehead. Some of the freckles were darker than others, smuts left by the city rain.

'Shit. Shit. Shit,' he said.

'Quite,' I replied, sitting comfortably on the bar stool and enjoying the first rush of tequila warming my face. 'So Dexter knows about Tommy pirating his tapes. What about Tony? Did you tell him about Tony?'

'Yes. Well, a dead guy isn't going to pirate any tapes, is he? I told Dexter you'd done a deal with his brother,' he said, and wiped his face.

'Thanks. And I'm sure Tony would like to thank you himself, personally,' I said.

'I told you, getting them interested in *my* tape . . . remember that, *my* tape . . . was an in. Now they have to answer the phone when I call, it's a point of contact. Anyway, you said St John took it in.'

'Yes, but I didn't mention Tony. I said I had a deal with Tommy.'

'Oh.'

Keith tried to look apologetic. 'Sorry,' he said.

'I asked him if Cheryl LeMat was walking out with Tommy Levi.'

'Oh?' Keith was interested now.

'He told me in his own special way that it was highly unlikely,' I said, and as I glanced up at the mirror, I saw the tall redhead go by. Her shiny hair was loose over a darted denim jacket, and high-waisted black lycra trousers extended the length of her enviable legs to what would be shoulder high on most women.

'Enemy agent at six o'clock,' I said, and Keith turned his head to the side.

Cheryl LeMat had her back to us. She had joined a chic crowd sitting round a large table by the piano. They greeted each other like geese, stretching their necks to one side and then the other of each other's painted faces. Keith slid his elbow off the bar and walked over. As soon as he had introduced himself, she took a step back from him. I could see her shaking her head, pushing her hair back from her face in exasperation. He said something, and tugged at her arm. She pulled it back. Then he leaned close to her and said something else, and she bit her lip and nodded before walking over towards the bar with him.

'Hi,' I said, taking another little sip of my marguerita.

She scowled at me and slid on to a seat on the other side of Keith.

'Drink?' said Keith.

She nodded, and asked for a Southern Comfort and ice. I

got another marguerita, and Keith paid without flinching.

'I can't tell you much,' she said, after taking a small taste of her drink.

'All right. Tell me why you telephoned the paper,' said Keith. Cheryl kept her head down, staring at her drink. Then she looked up at him, her large green eyes clear and cool as my tequila and lime.

'You wrote that Tommy had been selling those tapes before he died. I thought maybe it was true, maybe that's why he had died. I just got scared, that's all.'

She was lying. It was the hint of a challenge in her eyes that gave the game away. Keith was having none of it. 'Oh come on, Cheryl. I answered the telephone. You were serious. What was it? Did someone find out about you and Tommy? Was that it? Did you think Tommy had been murdered for you?'

She rattled the plastic stirrer around her glass, and her henna hair fell forward, covering her face. Pushing a bright-nailed hand through the red strands to raise it away from her smooth high forehead, she turned to him again for a second try. Her large eyes were wider now, open with sincerity, pleading to be believed. 'Look, Tommy was a sweet fun guy. When I found out he'd been killed, I thought someone had . . . come to the wrong conclusion about him and me. That's all.' She looked at me for support, as if I'd understand her situation.

'What made you change your mind?' I said.

'No one had come to any conclusion. I made a mistake. That's all. I made a mistake.'

I sighed, and took a swallow of my drink. Keith patted his pockets for a cigarette. He found some, and offered one to Cheryl first and then to me. We both accepted and waited for a light. She got hers first.

'Where'd Tommy get the tapes?' I said, before taking a deep breath of smoke. Her slender arm balanced on her elbow on the bar, the cigarette was between her fingers. It wasn't for smoking, it was just an accessory to emphasise the

103

length of her crimson nails.

'I don't know,' she said, looking at me straight, the challenge back in her green eyes.

'What about the photographs? And what about that printout?'

Her pale face tensed, but she didn't answer me. Keith was watching me now. I inhaled again and blew some smoke above our heads.

'The what?' she said after a few moments.

'Cheryl, I know whoever killed Tommy wasn't some supplier who thought he was a grass. Whoever killed him wanted one or all of four things: heroin, some wonderfully tasteful Polaroid shots of you, the tapes, "Seethru", "The Unreleased Johnny Waits" and the early Carla and Big one and a computer printout. The printout contained Ghea's sales figures. Never mind the smack, how did Tommy get the Ghea tapes, those photos and the printout? What do you know about them?'

Her wide red mouth contracted into a little wrinkled pip of anger. 'You stupid bitch, you don't understand a fucking thing,' she said, breaking her cigarette in two as she ground it hard into an ashtray. She tried to go, but Keith grabbed her arm and held it firm. His fingers squeezed hard. She looked around to see if anyone was watching. They weren't. 'He must have stolen them. He came to the house from time to time. Have you got them?'

'No,' I said. 'Didn't I say? Whoever killed Tommy took the lot.'

Now there was a different look in her wide eyes. It was a dark shiny look of fear. This girl knew who the killer was.

'Does that bother you?' I said.

Her terror was creeping over the bar to me, making the skin prickle on my head. She started to scratch the skin of her left hand, clawing at it rhythmically with her nails. 'I can't say any more. I've got to get out of here,' she said, looking over her shoulder and moving off the stool.

'Wait a minute. You've got to tell us. What's the big deal

104

with the printout?'

She rolled her eyes up in exasperation and her dark eyelashes curled up to her brows. Then she breathed out a terrible sigh of frustration before beginning again. 'Oh God. Let me go.'

'Will someone tell me what is going on?' said Keith. His voice was quiet, and a little higher than normal.

'Dexter was being blackmailed, is that it?' I said.

'Oh Christ, who's talking about Dexter?' she said, standing up and making to go. Keith couldn't hold her. She pushed herself away and walked straight out of the door.

'Now what?' said Keith. For once, the smug confident boyish look had disappeared. He looked older now, and serious.

'Another drink?' I said, raising my empty glass.

'Fuck you. Why didn't you tell me?'

'Because anything I tell you comes back at me like sick in the wind, Keith. I don't trust you, period. You use people. You're using her, and she's in trouble. What did you say to her in the first place, to get her to come over?'

Keith didn't answer. He slammed his drink down and walked briskly out of the door.

I looked down at my empty glass and called the lazy-eyed barman over. 'Do you accept any of the major credit cards?'

He smiled. 'Same again?' he asked, reaching for his silvery chrome shaker.

'Why not?' I said, smiling back. Two hours later, he called me a cab. Keith didn't return.

Chapter 9

I heard the doorbell ring. The bright blue luminescent glow of the digital clock radio said it was 4.53 a.m., and the grinding noise of traffic travelling north and south under the river reverberated beyond my window through the slush. It was still raining. My mouth was dry, and my head felt as if it weighed forty pounds. I could feel the membranes inside my mouth clinging to my teeth as I lay on my back and pulled the duvet over my face. I felt a bad moon arising. The bell rang again.

The door was pretty strong. Two-inch-thick reinforced steel, deadlocked and bolted, chained and manacled to the wall. Whoever was out there would have to call the fire brigade to get in. Hell, maybe the marines. The bell rang again. No thumping on the door. Just an anxious jabbing at the bell. It made me nervous. I lay there, trying to peel my eyes open. I wouldn't put a light on. I'd just creep over to the door and look through the spyhole. The light would be on in the hall. It would be OK. Yes, I could do that.

Quietly I eased my way out of bed and crawled on my hands and knees across the bedroom to the front room, which seemed to rock in the darkness. I clambered upright against the doorframe. The tequila that a few hours ago had added sparkle to my life was turning sour in my stomach. I tiptoed gently to the front door and trying not to breathe at all placed my eye up to the spyglass and tried to focus. It was hard to keep steady. The front of my head was so numb and congested that I could barely keep my eyelids open.

Keith was standing close to the door, with his arm resting on the doorframe by the bell. After about thirty seconds he stepped back. I could see his other arm now. It was bandaged round the wrist. His suit jacket wasn't hanging straight and there was a rip in the trousers, exposing a white bandage on his knee. He looked up and down the corridor and then turned to walk away. When he heard the bolts go, he started limping back quickly.

'Thanks . . . I'm sorry,' he said, as he hobbled past me, and I rebolted the door.

'You got the girl, then? Or did she get you?' I muttered, walking dizzily into the kitchen to get myself three glassfuls of water. He didn't answer. I poked my head back round the door, and he was slumped on my sofa, one leg bent, the other spread stiffly out. He was as pale as a chicken's egg, and his wet dark hair stuck to his face like weed. 'Tea or coffee?' I said wearily, thinking I could cope with that much hospitality, but he didn't answer. 'Keith?'

I went towards him, and he opened his eyes. There was a bloody red blot on the cornea close to the blue iris of his left eye. Dark shadows cut under his lower lids, and his lower lip was swollen and grazed to a shine like a bruised plum. He smelt of mushrooms. 'Tea,' he said, and closed his eyes again.

By the time I returned, his head was lolling heavily to one side. He didn't move as I sat next to him and placed the mugs on the table.

'Keith? Keith?' I shook his shoulder slightly. 'Drink this if you can. It's tea. It's hot.' He didn't answer, and I felt a small jolt of concern. 'Keith? Shall I call a doctor? Keith?'

He lifted his head to shake it, and with some effort held up a hand. He didn't want a doctor. He tried to speak, but his lips stuck together as he ventured to open his mouth. His voice was dry and weary. 'Wait a minute.'

He lay there a little longer with his eyes closed, and I lay back, too. I was almost asleep when he leaned forward with some difficulty and picked up his mug of tea with his good right hand. 'Ouch . . . God. I can't believe the X-ray didn't show up any broken ribs,' he said, taking a careful swallow.

I rubbed my hand across my eyes to dull the jabbing in my head. I wondered if his pain was worse than this. 'What happened?' I said, hardly looking at him.

'Someone ran me down.'

'What?'

'I'm not kidding. I followed Cheryl up the road. She was looking for a cab. She looks around, starts running, I step off the pavement to cross over – and wham, on my fucking back. Bastard didn't stop, didn't do anything, just put his foot down.'

'Did you get his number?'

Keith looked at me expressionlessly. 'Funny, that's what the police asked. There am I arse over tit in the gutter . . . Believe me, all I got to see was fucking stars.'

'Maybe he'd been drinking,' I said.

'Maybe.'

I squinted at him, protecting my eyes from the light. 'You shouldn't be here, you know. You should be in hospital, or at home, or maybe even a friend's house.'

Keith lay back with some effort, resting the mug between his legs. He smiled, and a little bead of red blood oozed like perspiration on to his swollen lower lip. 'There's no better way to a girl's heart than through a vein of pity, George. You still fancy me, don't you?'

It must be true. Men think about sex every fifteen minutes. Or was it fifteen seconds? Fifteen seconds. 'Wasn't she gorgeous?' he said, after a while.

'Absolutely. And very intelligent too.'

'You didn't even try to like her, that was the problem. You wound her up. You've got to go about these things with more subtlety, George.'

'Like you, you mean.'

'Exactly.'

We both lay slumped back with our eyes closed. I had no real energy for a fight.

'Do you think Carla had her? Yeah, I can understand Carla

wanting to get into her knickers . . . C'mon, did you fancy her? I did. Wouldn't mind showing her my box of tricks. You think she likes it straight or what?' he said.

We both opened our eyes and looked at each other. I was beginning to regret ever opening the door. His eyes closed again, and he smiled, like a lunatic sure of his own sanity.

'You're a sick man, Keith,' I said, and he sighed as he reached forward and took a painful swallow of tea. When he'd finished, I took the empty mug from his hands. The question now was, did he get my bed or the sofa? 'You'd better sleep in my room,' I said, getting up.

'Love to. But I won't be at my best, I warn you!' He grinned, his eyes half open now.

'Just forget it, Keith. Stop performing, for Christ's sake. You remind me of a circus seal,' I said, and turned to walk away from him.

Groaning and grunting, he lifted his legs up to lie full length where he was. 'This'll do nicely, m'dear,' he said, once he'd painfully lowered both his legs and closed his eyes again.

I was too weary to argue. I took a spare blanket from my room, and covered him. He looked deep asleep as I switched off the light, but as I walked through my bedroom door, he called out.

'It was a class 'mobile, though.

'What?'

'The bastard that hit me. Grey BMW 525i. Class, you know.'

I knew.

Though we'd slept until late morning, Keith didn't look too good. His eyes were puffy and his wrist was sore. My eyes were puffy, too.

'It's just a sprain. The knee's got eighteen stitches, but Christ, my ribs . . . ' He stretched a millimetre one side, then another, grimacing with pain.

I pushed a plate towards him. 'Eat some toast.'

'What are we going to do?'

'You're doing nothing. You're going to stay here and rest.'

'I need some clothes.'

'Yes, you do.'

He was sitting there, big-boned and skinny, in a pair of low-slung boxer shorts that hurt my eyes. Nothing grew on his chest, but a tough spiral of dark hair curled up his flat stomach and grasped his navel. His large ribs moved intact under the pale freckled skin that covered his long upper body and his wide shoulders. The long muscles of his arms and legs were smooth and strong-looking like those of a high jumper. For all his lankiness, Keith didn't look weak. He chewed carefully at the toast, and a little muscle popped in and out above his jaw. 'Let's share what we've got, George.'

'There isn't anything more.'

'Oh yeah? Look, together we can cover more ground. This story is going to make our names; we'll have cracked it. Then you'll be grateful. You'll want to thank me. Maybe you'll want to thank me a lot by making wild passionate love to me.'

'I can't imagine ever feeling that grateful, Keith. No, I'm not going to get conned by you again. Thanks very much.'

He rolled his eyes up, the red clot in his left eye giving him the air of a minor Catholic martyr. 'Come on! You still mad about that? You needed a kick up the ass. Wallowing around with your head up it. Come on . . . Admit it.'

'No.'

'OK, just as a show of good faith, I'll tell you what I know, OK? I just wished we'd put our heads together before we spoke to her. I had my money on Dexter.'

I still had. Maybe there was someone else, but Dexter was the man on the spot. I poured us both some more tea before leaning back in the kitchen chair with my eyes closed. The pain in my head was growing sharper like someone was twisting my hair into a fearsomely neat ponytail. The face of Wiggy's lazy-eyed barman mocked me, and I saw till-receipts bunched in a glass like celery. One too many,

110

no, many too many margueritas. I just never knew when to stop. No more. I couldn't do that again. I couldn't bear feeling like this again. No more. Never again.

Keith started to move his large good hand about in the air by way of supplementary explanation. 'Look, when I wrote that story, I didn't really believe Tommy Levi had died because of the tapes.'

'So why did you run the story?'

'I wanted to stir Dexter up.'

'Why?'

'Carla.' He put the crust of his toast on the side of his plate and brushed a crumb delicately from his scabby lip. 'I think he killed her. She didn't take hard drugs, period. So I got to thinking about who would benefit from her death.'

'Her estate.'

'Sure, if the contract says so. Any contract she signed lives, unless it's specifically written in that upon death it reverts automatically to the estate. The record company gets a phenomenal boost in sales but the *manager*, who will also have signed a management contract, carries on getting 25 per cent for managing the estate. He can do what he likes, and there's so much you can do in terms of merchandising when someone dies.'

'The manager?'

'Yes. Not just Dexter. He and St John both gain.'

Keith lit a cigarette over the empty plates and offered me one, which I refused. Little glands were pumping saliva under my tongue. I felt my throat tighten, and I had to swallow to keep my breakfast down.

'I'd like to see the printout that Tommy Levi died for. I'd like to see what's in it, wouldn't you?' he said.

'Well, Tony Levi's seen it, and he says it's a bunch of Ghea's sales and marketing figures,' I replied unenthusiastically.

'That's interesting . . . ' Keith sipped at some tea and thought for a while.

'Why?' I said.

111

'Why'd they want it back?'

I shrugged. It was an effort to think.

'Well, listen to this . . . When Johnny Waits died, his old hit "Cover me (I want your love)" – the one we sampled – went to number one for eight weeks. His all-time best-selling album "Here's Johnny!", which had dropped out of the top one hundred charts for the first time that year, re-entered the top twenty. So, just by dying he had added fifteen thousand additional sales in a week. Carla got lucky, too, of course. I know because Mick and I got lucky for a change. "Why doncha (cover me . . .)?" popped right back into the charts again alongside that single from her first album, "A Night Drive". They were both selling ten thousand copies a week. Ghea made a fortune from Waits dying. And Ghea and St John are doing the same with Carla, especially if her contract doesn't revert. I had a word with Mike Dome, Ghea's new contract for the Dudes . . .'

'Doesn't revert.'

'Right. And who was with Waits and Carla when they died?'

'Dexter.'

'Right.'

It was all a bit much to absorb in my weakened state. I had to consider that Keith might be hallucinating from the blow to his head.

He sucked at his cigarette, and carried on talking quickly and excitedly. 'Cheryl LeMat knows who's doing it. She was shitting herself last night. We know Dexter and St John both gain. Let's say Dexter killed Carla and Waits. Now we know that someone wanted that report back off Tommy and everything else he'd taken. And it wasn't her husband. She said so. So who is it? It's got to be St John. The stuff got nicked from his place. Get it? That's what that was all about last night. She thinks . . . She *knows* St John knocked Tommy off. I know she knows. When she rang me up, she was really upset. I mean really. She wasn't thinking. Then she clammed up because she started wondering what he'd do to her if he found out she had tried to tell someone. Last night, she just backtracked because she was scared. I mean, you know the guy, wouldn't you be? She knows what's in that report. She gave it to Tommy, or he stole it while he was with her. Now she's scared that if St John killed Tommy and got the stuff back, he must know that she's to blame for the whole mess in the first place, and that she's been cheating on him. He's giving her one, I'm sure of it. And if that report shows up just how profitable death in this business can be, he and Dexter won't want anyone else to see it. That's the story, I'll stake my life on it.'

'How'd she get to know Tommy?'

'He's a pusher. She's a junkie. He may have got payment in kind, or maybe she just wanted a little fun with him.'

Oh yes. Poor Cheryl. I thought about her standing between Dexter and St John at the party, twisting the glass round and round. St John introduced her, not Dexter, and on the phone he didn't like hearing my suggestion about her and Tommy. I didn't realise how close I'd been. She was beautiful and messed up. She was happiest with heroin and straps tied to her naked flesh. How can someone so beautiful lose like that? Why not? The more beautiful and the more talented, the more vulnerable, because everyone can see what they've got to lose. Poor Carla. My poor friend Carla living with these people. As she had said herself, death was a career move in this business. Keith could be right. I clutched my forehead with my hand. My brains were slopping against my skull like water in a ship's bucket, and my throat was beginning to tighten again, squeezing the back of my tongue. Keith took a final long drag on his stubby cigarette and winced as it stuck to his lip. I didn't say anything, and rose wearily to my feet to get him a tissue as he dabbed gently at the ooze round his mouth.

'What do you think?' he said, looking up at me.

I shrugged. 'You can't plan how a star's death is going to affect people. It's more than sales of records and blockbuster tours. Loads of singers and bands are so-called

113

megastars, but if they died tomorrow, it'd be "Ooh, what a shame" and then business as usual. They have to have some . . . some empathy with a generation or an age. They have to be charismatic. Like James Dean. Like Monroe. Like Lennon. Now if Dylan died tomorrow, I agree, the record company would probably make as much on him in three weeks as they've done in the past five years. But they'd have probably made more if he'd died ten years ago when he was still doing good stuff. How'd they know when someone should die? They have to see the future.'

'Well, Waits was back in the public eye. He was a success again.'

'Yes, but your theory falls down with Carla. She was an up and coming star.'

'Perhaps she'd already up and comed, if "Seethru" was anything to go by. Thought of that?'

I stood next to him, arms folded. He had a point, but he didn't have all the facts.

'Keith, dear, your theory's good but it isn't so neat. Tony Levi has a grey BMW 525i. How does that fit in?'

He raised his eyebrows and tried to smile. 'Oh, that's interesting, isn't it?' he said, and then he winked his blooded eye. 'What a story, Georgina! Can you believe this is happening to us?'

'Excuse me,' I said, and hurried to my windowless bathroom, my mouth tight shut.

Keith wasn't too pleased when I told him that I didn't feel well and was going back to bed. He wanted action. He wanted us to plan our next moves. I wanted to crush my head between two pillows and sleep, perchance to die. If I lived, then I wanted to talk to Tony Levi, alone. I set the alarm for 1.30 p.m. and awoke feeling hungry. Keith had gone. He'd left a note on the table in the front room. 'Gone home to change. Call you later.'

I went into the kitchen, opened the fridge and took out the tough little square of Cheddar that rested in isolation on the second shelf. I put two slices of white bread under the grill and gnawing at the hard unyielding chunk of cheese, looked out at the damp, drab, grey Sunday that presented itself from my sixth-floor kitchen window. God, how many times had I done this on my own? Carla had said to me once that I hadn't moved on. She was right. What was I getting out of hard lonely drinking and hangovers that lasted a day? What was I getting out of this grubby place? I felt defeated, wearied by Keith's eager energy, and so tired. Did I really care now? Did I really want to trawl through all the rottenness? Keith was no different from the rest of them, wanting something out of Carla's death: a little bit of fame. What did I want? Justice. Come on. What did I really want? I wanted peace. I wanted to wipe all this nightmare away. I didn't want it to be nearly Christmas. I didn't want to see the little plastic decorations and seasonal spray snow appearing in the windows of the tower blocks like rows of cheap cards. I wanted the world to be light and warm. I wanted it to be summer with flies and flowers. I wanted to talk to Carla again. I wanted to change my mind, tell her that I'd go on the tour with her, be her friend. Watch those people, those men around her. Get her home, alive. I could have done that. What would it have cost? I could have explained to her how I wanted it to be. If I had done that instead of expecting her to know, would things have been different now? She'd sent me a message and postcards saying 'Wish you were here', and I'd been embarrassed by them. I felt ashamed now.

The smell of burning toast began to creep over me. I jumped and dragged the pan out from under the grill, tipping the charred husks into the sink. The yellow flames rapidly damped out under a rush of water from the tap, and billows of dark smoke rose to obscure the window and fill the room. My hand stung where I'd caught it on the hot grill, the skin lifted up like paper and, underneath, it was whitened and dry like cooked chicken. I stood stiffly by the table, holding on to a chair, my heart beating hard, rattled by this minor domestic disaster. I pulled out the chair and sat down slowly, covering my face with my hands as if to shut out the unbearable misery I now felt. It was so lonely here, I was so alone, and it was my fault. I couldn't surrender one inch of ground. I couldn't compromise. Not with my husband, not with my friends, not with anyone. This was the result. They'd all gone. There was just me, the perfect proud individualist. The perfect fool trudging along, morning until night, me and a bottle of something. And now, if it didn't beat all, my hand stung and my breakfast was burnt.

The silence in the flat made me aware that I had begun shouting and sobbing out loud, howling at myself in my little oblong kitchen. Gradually I stopped, and feeling foolish, looked about. No demons stood in the corners. I was still alone, and the twisting pain had gone from my chest. I walked into the bathroom, filled a basin full of warm water and splashed the water over my face. I looked up at the mirror. It was OK. I could call Tony Levi now. It was OK.

I dialled. He answered the phone. He said he'd wait for me at his pub that evening, but I said No, I had another pub in mind. I wanted him off his territory and on mine; a little pub in West Ham where the landlord knew me. I'd even worked behind the bar once or twice when he'd been busy, so I thought that if Tony tried anything, he'd help me out. The venue had another plus point: the landlord's dog was the only one allowed on the premises.

I didn't hear from Keith again that day, so I dozed the afternoon away on the sofa while the television entertained me with the omnibus edition of some television soap I didn't follow, three animal-crushing cartoons and an hour of American football. I drank a lot of tea and had a bath. My scorched hand stung, but my head didn't hurt any more. Put it this way, I didn't feel like I'd been the one hit by a 525i.

By 7.30 p.m., I was dressed and ready to go. I wore all black, what else? A polo-necked jumper, above-the-knee skirt, leggings, shiny leather pointed bootees that pinched my toes, all chain-store and market-stall stuff except for the cropped tan suede jacket that had cost me a lot of money up

West. I imagined myself wearing little black leather gloves, driving a BMW. No, not me. I'd need little tan all-leather brogues, a bob of straight, shiny, honey-coloured hair and a straight Aryan nose to be credible. I slicked on some bronze-coloured lipstick and blew myself a kiss. It wasn't raining, so I could walk up the road and get a minicab.

Chapter 10

Tony arrived at 8.30 sharp, but I'd been there half an hour, early enough to get a seat away from the pub's blazing real log fire. The chimney-breast glittered with horse brasses and cheap tinsel decorations that spread, draped and roped across the walls and from the Tudor-style beamed ceiling like gaudy garlands on an Indian elephant.

Tony saw me sitting in the corner, nodded, and stepped up to the bar. The landlord's face was stretched happily in an irregular grin of welcome. I felt sick. The pair obviously knew each other. Tony bought him a drink, and motioned to me. I shook my head and raised my glass, clear with untainted tonic water. The landlord's Dobermann pinscher had scampered round the bar and was nosing Tony's leg and waggling its flat brown bottom with happiness.

'I suppose you know everyone, do you?' I said, as he took the seat opposite.

'You mean old Arthur? He follows the boxing, that's all. Your local, is it?'

'Sometimes. Were you that good, then?'

'Not good enough.'

I felt uncomfortable. He had to be thinking why I'd chosen this place nestling in a cubic wasteland of industrial premises and council flats when I could just as easily have met him at the discreet Salmon and Ball. He didn't ask. He just leaned over to take a drink of beer from his over-full half, and wiping the froth from his dark lips said, 'Well, how was your day?' I told him that I'd slept for most of it. 'You go out last night?'

'Funny you should ask. Yes, I did, and I picked up some very interesting information.'

'Oh?'

He sat back in the red-padded vinyl half-barrel chair, placed the ankle of one lean elegant leg on the knee of the other and chewed a little at his clean manicured thumb. I thought of St John and his thumb-gnawing habit. Tony made it look stylish. Two punters at the bar began to sing that they wished it could be Christmas every day, forgot the rest of the lyric and la-lad to some sort of finale. Arthur was laughing.

'I don't think Dexter's your man. He might be mine, but he's not yours. He didn't kill Tommy,' I said.

'But you still think he killed Carla, yeah? Cheryl tell you anything more?'

The perspiration started under my arms and I was warm enough to smell my own perfume. I slid my jacket off and looked in my bag for a cigarette. He wasn't even going to pretend.

'She told us it wasn't Dexter who wanted the stuff back. She was pretty scared. She knows who Tommy's murderer is, for sure, but it isn't Dexter.'

'Who, then?'

'St John. John St John. Carla's manager.'

Tony flicked at the niggling snag of nail on his thumb and turned to see Arthur making his way over to us with a couple of drinks. The two singers had recognised Tony, and sent over their tribute. I wished I'd picked somewhere else for the showdown. Arthur gave me a little nod, and chatted to Tony for a while about upcoming events at the town hall and a middleweight contest scheduled for Wembley. Tony smiled and nodded. He was almost charming.

When Arthur had shuffled off, I began again. 'You were there, Tony, weren't you? What did you see?' I said, extracting a cigarette from a fresh packet. My nasty tone didn't ruffle him, and he didn't answer. 'So where did you take her?'

He pushed a hefty glass ashtray towards me and picked up

119

a beer-mat. He placed it at the edge of the table and flicked it over, catching it neatly in his hand. He repeated the trick as he spoke. 'I didn't take Cheryl anywhere. Geezer picked her up. It weren't her old man either . . . I've seen him. It was definitely the bloke in the photos, I recognised him. Took some doing 'n all, considering the light, the dodgy angles and the fact that he was bollock naked then. Bit of a gorilla. He cuffed her about the head a couple of times and then stuck his tongue down her throat. True love and all that.'

'Oh, charming.'

'Yeah. Amazing what you girls like, ain't it?'

I stared hard at him. 'Oh yes. Amazing what we don't like, but get anyway.'

He shook the fingers of his hand as if they'd been stung. He was laughing at me.

'So where was Keith during all this?' I said.

Tony began sliding his thumb and forefinger up and down his trouser-leg. His dead eyes glittered to the dancing flames of Arthur's real log fire. 'He was about five yards down the road, giving out in the gutter,' he said.

The Dobermann sat by the fire and looked over at Tony every now and then with an expression of unbridled affection. What was it with these animals? My mother had always said if animals, dogs in particular, like someone, you could too, and *vice versa*. My dog Timmy had always been able to spot a villain, unlike his mistress. But now that I was older I wanted a more convenient form of social litmus paper. I didn't want to walk through life with a dog on a leash testing for trouble like a miner's canary. Anyway, I wasn't sure about Arthur's dog's judgment right now.

'And where were you?' I said.

'Idling in me motor, watching, playing with me carphone . . .' He breathed out a little contemptuous laugh, and I shook my head.

'You're a bastard, you know that?'

Tony's mouth closed on a sarcastic smile before he

120

continued. '. . . Calling an ambulance. Should have called one for you 'n all,' he finished.

'Oh, the good Samaritan now, are we? How touching.'

'What's the problem? Disappointed with the shape he's in?'

I was beginning to lose my temper, and so was he. 'I know what you did. Keith saw your car,' I said. 'He didn't know it was you. He was following Cheryl, and you hit him. Damn near killed him. Why? What's going on?'

'How'd you figure that?' Tony was sitting forward now and pulling at his ear-lobe.

'Keith saw the car. It was a grey 525i. Just like yours, remember?'

'Registration?'

'No.'

'No? Lucky I was there then, weren't it? Unique kind of number. The sort that flash bastards stick on their cars to save you troubling your friends down the nick. JSJ 100. Initials familiar at all?'

Oh God, they were. 'He's got a 525i?' I said. Tony nodded. 'Last time I saw him, he had a Jag.'

'Well, he's got a 525i now with a little dent in the front.'

'He just drove the car at him?'

'Well, he was sort of pissed off. Didn't like your boyfriend feeling up his girl. Jealous type, got to watch them, know what I mean?'

How right he was. I was a jealous type, but with no follow-through. I knew the plans that could be wrought, the deadly little punishments oiled by the bitter taste of retribution. I knew the black madness of envy. It could have been funny. Big bad St John in love. Senseless with it. Killing for it. The meanest son of a bitch in the universe being pulled this way and that by a ring through his nose. I could just see his face the night he found out that the tapes, the report, the photographs had gone. A dumb beast's face puffing and blowing stormy mucus through its flared nostrils. Tommy must have come back to him for money, and he knew then. He knew how he'd got the stuff. Cheryl LeMat had let him take her, and then take everything, but St John still loved her. St John, the rock and roll minotaur with his short legs and barrel-chest, hopelessly, achingly in love with the lissom, lovely, catwalk goddess Cheryl LeMat. Taking photographs of their lovemaking so he could believe it was true afterwards, that it was him bobbing like a cheap shiny beach-ball in the glorious red stream of her hair.

'Well, what are you going to do?' I said, the cigarette now hanging, still unlit, from my mouth. Tony said nothing. I struck a match under my cigarette and inhaled deeply. I wondered why Keith hadn't told me the whole story. So much for sharing. Was he an angle ahead of me in this chase? 'Look, let's call the police. Tell them about Tommy. Tell them the story about Tommy and Cheryl LeMat.'

Tony got to his feet and gathered up the glasses. 'We shifted four grands' worth of your tape last week. The punters love it. Looks like we won't be short for Christmas.'

He was making a point. Small beer when you thought about one tape, but Tony had built a business around more than one tape and who knows what else. I wondered how much money he made in a week. St John had said thousands, millions in a year, more than some record companies.

'What about Dexter? He won't let us get away with it now the tape belongs to Ghea,' I said, when he came back with a half pint of beer for himself and another clear bubbling tonic water for me.

'Let him tell the old Bill what we're up to. I don't think we got no worries about that,' he said, and sat down.

'Tony, look, I'm not really interested in that any more. I'm not sure why I brought the tape to you in the first place. Maybe I was looking for a story, maybe I wanted to poke Ghea in the eye, whatever, but I don't think I wanted money. It's not important to me any more, but I want an investigation into Carla's death, at least.'

He looked unsympathetic. 'Look, *we* can't tell them, all right? We don't know nothing yet.'

'Keith's got a theory,' I replied.

'Oh yeah?' The very mention of Keith provoked a great wall of East End contempt in Tony. 'You trust this Keith?' he said, stretching both legs in front of him and folding his hands over his groin.

I looked over at him. Nothing. No help. 'Not really,' I said. 'He's a journalist, isn't he?'

Tony smiled, but didn't show his teeth. 'So are you, and I trust you, don't I?'

I felt my cheeks burn. 'I'm flattered, but I'm not a journalist any more.'

'Yeah. And I ain't a boxer any more, but I still know how to fight.'

I looked away from him. We'd finally said something about each other. My cheeks were burning. They always let me down. How could I be cool with my face lit up like a log fire? Had he paid me a compliment? I'd felt more confident with his antagonism. It gave me something to push against.

'You like him?' he said.

'I do and I don't. He can be a pain. Yes, I do like him, I suppose, and I don't like to see him hurt.'

We sat in silence, Tony looking over at me while I scattered my gaze about the room. In his room, I'd felt an odd feeling of redundancy when he'd finished speaking; that the session was over and that I could leave. Here, I got the feeling that we were more equal, a partnership. Maybe he didn't frighten me any more, or maybe he just wasn't trying so hard.

'All right. What's the theory?' he said at last.

'OK. This is going to sound ridiculous, but it isn't if you think about it and what's happened. Keith reckons that Dexter and St John benefited from Waits's and Carla's deaths. Unless the contract says so specifically, upon death the manager and the record company carry on coining it in for the life of the contract as if the artists were alive. In any case, he thinks they planned they'd gain more sales short term from the rush of punters to the shops on account of the

123

deaths of Waits, and Carla, than they would have done if the pair had kept on performing long term. He thinks Waits and Carla died to make Ghea and St John a profit.'

'Keith worked this out?'

'Yes. It's incredible, I know – and I don't see what it's got to do with Tommy – but somehow it makes a crazy sort of sense. The only thing I can't understand is why Carla. She was in her prime.'

Tony sucked in his breath and let out a sigh. 'Depends what the software said about her, I suppose,' he said, and I knew for sure then that Keith was on to something.

Tony didn't want to talk about it in Arthur's pub. I had to go with him. Whether I trusted him or not, he'd baited the hook too well. Now we were getting somewhere. Arthur saw us leave, called out and gave us a cheery gold-fingered wave. The dog stood up as we left. 'Merry Christmas, you lovely people! Be lucky,' he said, as Tony held open the door for me to pass.

'Yeah, be lucky, Arthur. All right?' Tony called back as I stood outside in the cold. Goodnight, Arthur, and thank you for your support.

Tony edged the car out into the dark main road, which led past a shuttered stranded dance hall and an empty Chinese take-away to a busy sodium-lit dual carriageway that raced down from the Bow flyover. The car weaved through the winking traffic-cones dividing the lanes.

'Hungry?'

'Yes,' I said.

'Steak?'

'I fancy a Macdonalds.' I was thinking of the comforting bright lights and the big glass windows of the red-and-gold hamburger palace.

Tony gave a little laugh. 'You're a cheap night out, aincha?'

'Maybe, but who said you were paying?' I said roughly, and we chose not to speak again until we got to East Ham.

The place was almost empty. We queued up together, and

Tony took the tray of food and drink to a table away from the window but facing the door while I dug into my purse for the money. We unwrapped the cartons, still without saying a word.

'Relax,' he said, after swallowing a wet bite of a Big Mac and running his tongue over his wet lips.

I put my hamburger down. 'I can't. Tell me, now.'

He took another bite, and I waited as he chewed slowly and swallowed again. This time he wiped the napkin round his mouth and looked up. 'From what I saw of the printout, it was only Johnny Waits's sales. Not Carla's. It was econometric trend analysis, yeah? You understand that?'

'Yes, I do, but forgive me if I say I'm surprised that you do.'

'Yeah, well . . . My bet is that they're using a stats package to analyse all the marketing variables against sales and then do a forecast. Maybe they stuck an expert system on the front end to come to some conclusions. Database and spreadsheet calculations with an extra edge? What do you think?'

I thought he knew more about the little boxes than he'd let on, and let him continue. 'What you do is build up a computer model of previous deaths and subsequent sales, so the computer can look back for a pattern. Circumstantial evidence, but it points us in the right direction, don't it?'

He was a clever boy.

'Like your mate Keith says, they've made death a marketing issue. The software takes everything into account and says when to terminate a product for maximum returns. That's what it said. It's there in the figures. Johnny Waits had to die November 1988 for maximum returns. It's not that difficult to do with a machine, you see, you just got to be a wicked bastard to want to. Remember the six-month comeback to remind everyone of how great he was, and then . . .'

'Why didn't you tell me this in the first place?' I said. He shrugged. 'Come on!'

'Look, I didn't, all right?'

'No, it's not.'

He took a few french fries from his carton. 'You got a temper, aincha?' he said, before feeding the fries into his mouth.

I closed my eyes for a count of ten. 'Do you think they put it to work on Carla?' I said.

The look he gave me was something akin to pity. 'If they did it for Waits, why not her? Why not every potential loser on their books. Why wait five or ten years for a comeback? Why spend millions so that some one-hit wonder can rediscover themselves on one of them difficult second albums that takes three years to produce and doesn't have one good tune on it?'

'I can't believe it.'

'Yeah, well. What d'you think? Think real business is full of Albert Schweitzers? You never heard of corporate crime? These big companies are making profit-only decisions all the time – powdered milk for third world babies, factories that leak poisons, drugs that deform babies, cars with petrol tanks that explode if someone gives you a little fender-bender shunt up the backside. What d'you think – the worst thing in the world is pirating a tape?' He took a final bite of what was left of his burger. I had made slower progress. 'Eat,' he said.

'They'll junk it, won't they?' I said, picking at my fries.

'Well, they might do if they think we're on to them. This John St John knows I've seen the report. He's got the tapes back. He knows you know me. I think Dexter's got to be working with him on this program, but does he know he's humping his wife?'

'That's a point. Does Dexter know that the report went missing in the first place?' I said.

Tony shrugged again. 'Maybe, maybe not. We know he knew the tapes had gone missing, because of you. He knew you knew the pirate, Tommy. And your mate has told him you were pirating the new tape just to confirm things. But the report, the photos . . . I don't know. If St John killed Tommy, he has them back now. But would he tell Dexter?

Tell him that the report went out of his hands, but it's all right now 'cos he's got it back.'

Now I took a bite of my hamburger and chewed over that and what I knew. I'd never been a good judge of men that I cared about, but I was pretty good at assessing men that I didn't. St John wouldn't, couldn't, have panicked like that. And he wouldn't do things that way. He was the horned sort that wanted his victims alive, to feel pain. He wouldn't let anyone die and get away from him like that. He'd want to see them walking around afterwards, suffering, stumbling, broken to pieces. But I'd only seen him in business. Maybe, in love, he was different, mellower.

'I still can't believe St John killed Tommy,' I said.

'Well, he ran your boyfriend over, didn't he?'

'He didn't kill him, though.' I ignored the dig.

'No, but maybe that was an accident.'

'Very funny.' I wanted to ask why Tony had been hanging around last night, anyway. He'd seen me come out of Wiggy's and maybe seen Keith come to my place. Was he following me or Keith? Didn't he ever sleep? Why did Keith bother him so much? Maybe he didn't like Keith's bright ideas. 'Did you follow me last night?' I said.

'Yeah.'

'Why?'

'I told you. You and I have a problem now with these geezers wondering how much we know. If someone turns up, I'd like to know who.' He wasn't bothered whether I liked it or not. The answer was too pat, and I wasn't sure if I believed him.

'Protecting me, or just checking me out? Why didn't you give me a lift? Could have saved me the fare.'

'Didn't want you puking up in my car.'

'O ye of little faith,' I said, reaching for my bag and my cigarettes again. 'Did you watch my place, too, from down there in the car park? I'm touched. Really I am. Some people really get off on that sort of thing, but Keith isn't my boyfriend, you must know that by now.'

'So?'

'So why are you hanging around my door?'

He caught my right hand with his left. His grip was strong, and I winced. That made him twist my hand palm downwards slowly and easily. The burn from the grill pan had left a purple weeping weal of peeling skin below my knuckles. 'What you done to your hand?'

I tugged to get my fingers away, but he held fast and then, when he was ready, he released me.

'Burnt toast. Can't keep your eye on every damned thing,' I said, suddenly embarrassed that he might think I'd done it while I was drunk.

'You want to get that seen to. Looks as if it might turn nasty.'

I nodded cautiously, and we both rose to go.

'Are you going to kill him, Tony?' I said, as we stood by the car.

He waited, and then he laughed, like he wanted to tease me. 'Who?'

'Don't laugh. St John.'

'Nah, it's going to be much worse than that,' he said, and opened the door for me.

Everyone knew that everyone else knew, a little, at least. The question was what were we all going to do next? It was gone ten, and Tony had offered to drive me home. I didn't want to go with him. I wished that I had my own car so I could drive down to the river, walk, take in some damp cold air and think a little bit now that my head was clear. But I didn't have a car, so Tony escorted me to the door and checked the flat out. Then he gave me a courteous nod and walked down the hall. 'Thanks for supper,' he said, raising a hand, his back to me. He was half-way to the lift when I called out.

'Wait, Tony, I've got an idea. Please, if you've got a moment, come and look at these. I want to know what you think.'

Once inside, Tony stood behind me and stared at the dusty boxes that my old friend Warren had left behind with a stack of manuals on three shelves above the computer. Every one was labelled. Warren was so neat and thorough, too neat for me.

'The guy whose flat this used to be left me all these. He was a hacker. Liked writing little programs and breaking into big computers. Good at it, he was. Probably still is, if he hasn't given up. He made enough to retire on . . . Now where are they? Ah!'

Tony had to step back to avoid me crushing his feet as I turned round. I blew and brushed the dust off the grey box in my hand on to the front of his dark cashmere sweater. Before I knew it, my anxious hand was brushing the fluff from his chest. He looked down and took my wrist, gently lifting my hand off. 'Get on with it,' he said.

'I'm sorry.' I fumbled open the box. 'Look, this disk has got "Willy's Wild Ride" on it.'

'Yeah?'

'Yes. And in addition to this excellent game of pursuit, there is something else.'

'A virus.'

'Something like that, only it doesn't just replicate itself to clog up the system, it hijacks the system software for its own purposes. You into pirate software too, Tony?'

'Maybe.'

'Well, Warren either wrote or acquired this little program. He built up his collection of so-called logic bombs, Trojan Horses and viruses so he could take the little programs apart and analyse them, just in case he ever got one. He used bulletin boards a hell of a lot, a risky business nowadays if you want to download software, because so much public domain software is infected. You have to be able to recognise a virus, you see, before you get rid of it. Hence the little library here.'

'I see.'

'Well, Willy's little extra program can be set up to alter

129

system commands. Originally it was a little anti-copying software device for protecting against program piracy. If anyone tried to copy a master disk, a little trashing routine would come into play and wipe out the perp's hard disk for him. Now, this little program is a modification of that. It can be set up so that every time the computer receives a delete command, it ignores it and instead copies the information to however many computers on the network I suggest. Imagine the sort of chaos that would cause on a network?'

'Not nice.'

'No. But Ghea isn't nice either, is it? With this, I can trap Dexter. Once this is in the system and set up, if Dexter tries to wipe his files, he's finished. Staff all over the building will see the report, and he won't have time to analyse or stop the virus/logic bomb, call it what you like, it'll be too late by then. It'll expose him and give me time to get the police over there. I presume he has a network, of course. If so, it'll be easy to access him at arm's length, so to speak, through someone else's pc. If not, we have to get it on to his personal machine.'

Tony said nothing. He wasn't happy about the police.

'Well, the Johnny Waits report is going to get them thinking. I'm going to tell the police about it, Tony. I have to.'

'I told you . . .' he said, but I held up my hand.

'It won't affect us, I'm sure.'

Tony took the disk and walked away. He put it down on the coffee-table and turned round. He was waiting to see what I wanted him to do.

'First,' I said, 'we have to get someone to load up "Willy's Wild Ride" on to Ghea's network, so what I want to know, Tony, is how many reliable moles you have in there.'

His eyes widened, and then he started to laugh. It was a good honest-to-God laugh. I could see his teeth and two gold fillings, his healthy pink tongue. It was Tommy's laugh. I smiled at him. He wasn't too bad at all when he loosened up. Then he stopped. There was a persistent electronic whining sound coming from outside.

'My car,' he yelled, and as I ran to the window, he ran for

the door.

The whining stopped. I saw a flicker of light down below in the half-lit darkness and there was a hard crack, like a small explosion. Tony's 525i was ablaze.

Chapter 11

When the fire engine left, the little crowd of cheering onlookers coming home from the pub dispersed, leaving Tony and me gazing silently at the smoking wreck of the BMW.

'Looks pretty final,' said a voice behind us.

We turned, and saw Keith pay off a cab driver and stiffly straighten up. Tony said nothing. He glanced at Keith, and back at his burnt-out car. There were going to be no more laughs from Tony now.

'You guys want coffee? Come on, Tony. You can use my phone,' I said, and walked away from them towards the sour-smelling entrance of the dimly-lit block.

There wasn't much chat as I busied myself in the kitchen. Tony sat in what was now his usual seat, and Keith was back on the sofa. I thought Tony would have been eager to leave. He didn't like Keith. He could have called his cab firm and gone straight away. We'd said what we had to say, and he knew what I wanted him to do with the disk I had shown him. When I came out of the kitchen with the coffee, the atmosphere was distinctly unsociable. I felt like the chaperon for a snake and a mongoose.

'It must have been kids,' I said to a silent Tony Levi as I sat at the opposite end of the sofa to Keith.

'Yeah.'

'What was it? A BMW?' enquired Keith with ugly innocence.

'Yeah.'

'Nice car,' Keith replied, nodding with enthusiastic approval.

A bad situation was developing. I turned to him. 'Keith, Tony didn't hit you last night. It was St John. Tony saw it happen and called the ambulance. It seems Chery LeMat's St John's mistress. Didn't like you rubbing up against her, dear.'

'I wasn't anywhere near her, the bastard. He's crazy.'

Keith looked at Tony, who didn't bother to look up. He had rested one ankle on his knee and was running his thumb and forefinger up and down the crease of his trouser-leg. Keith winced with pain as he searched uncomfortably for his cigarettes and handed them round. Tony refused with a flick of his palm. The room was silent again but for the inhaling of cigarettes and the placing and replacing of coffee-mugs on the table.

Keith edged over nearer to me and pressed the stub of his cigarette down into the ashtray by my cup. 'Tony Levi. Tony Levi the boxer?' he said, looking up from under a couple of dark strands of hair. There was no response from Tony. 'You were good,' he continued, leaning back and swinging his good right arm over the back of the sofa behind me. 'ABA welterweight champion, unbeaten in ten professional fights. Pity about Robbie Slater, though.'

Tony's unblinking eyes watched him, dark as hammers.

Keith was sitting too close to me now. His arm was resting on the sofa behind my head, his fingers were resting on my shoulders. 'Did he ever regain his sight?' he said to Tony.

'No.'

Keith and his damned research. I wished I had done some before now. Keith was working him with what he knew.

'You were right, Keith,' I said quickly. 'What you said, that's what the report was about. Tony reckons they've got a computer on the job.'

'No shit? And Carla?'

'Nothing about Carla.'

'They must have something on her.'

'Yes, but would you hang on to something like that? You'd get rid of it, wouldn't you? Especially if you suspected someone knew.'

Keith looked excited now. Excited that he'd been right, excited about his story, even if he couldn't prove it. 'St John killed your brother, for sure, so St John has to have that report. We've got to get it back,' he said to Tony.

'Maybe we won't be able to,' I replied.

'He had a motive. We have to get into his place, see if he's got the stuff . . .'

'Well, thanks to you and your little tape, he's a little surer about who's on his trail, Keith. It's going to be a little more complicated than that now.'

Keith looked frustrated, and nothing more was said. I wanted them both to leave, but neither made any attempt to move. When I rose to take the cups into the kitchen, I wanted to be alone for a moment, but Keith followed me.

'Is he staying?' he whispered, as I loaded the crockery into the sink.

'What's it to you?'

'I don't trust him, that's all. He's a crook.'

'That's funny. I don't think he trusts you either,' I said.

'Do you?'

I turned and looked at him. 'What?'

'Trust me.'

'What do you think? Your form isn't good, Keith.'

'You stupid bitch! You've got to trust me. We can crack this thing, but we've got to be careful. Listen, I care about you. Kiss me. Like you kissed me in the rain. But mind the lip.' His face bent over mine, but I ducked under and out of the way.

'You jerk!' I whispered, and he started to laugh.

'Aw . . . still Carla's girl?' he said. I didn't answer. He raised an eyebrow, and one-handedly pulled out his cigarettes, flicked open the pack and put one to his mouth in an easy motion. 'I've got a better idea. I think we can pressure Cheryl into helping us out.'

'How's that?' The voice came from Tony in the doorway, who stood, hands in pockets. He looked small, dark and compact. Keith had filled the frame with his height.

'She's so shit scared she'll do anything if she thinks it'll help her get away from St John. She knows he's a murderer. She's too scared of him to leave, but she might help stitch him up. So I'll talk to her. She trusts me,' Keith replied. No one answered him. 'Someone has to handle Dexter, though,' he added, looking at me.

'I will,' I said quickly.

Tony turned away into the front room, and I followed him. He picked up the telephone receiver and pressed some numbers on the dial. 'Yeah. Ten minutes. You know it? Yeah. Bow.'

I handed him the disk. He took it. We were standing close together now. Keith had stayed in the kitchen. I knew he'd be trying to listen. 'How long will it take?' I said.

'Tomorrow morning do you?'

'Fine. Then what are you going to do?'

'I'll be in touch. Don't tell him.'

'Why?'

'It's your story, ain't it?'

'Tony . . .'

I heard Keith sink into the sofa with a grunt, but Tony was already walking past me to where he had been sitting. We waited for the cab's horn to sound, and then he left.

'Nice guy,' said Keith, as I shut the door.

'You are a shit, Keith! Do you know that?'

'Look, that bastard ran me over last night. I know it. He was in a hurry, trying to keep up with her. He must have followed her and seen her with St John. He's the shit, I'm telling you. I just feel like it.'

'That why you burned his car?'

Keith looked at me in surprise, and then began to snigger. 'How'd you guess?'

'I've used the cab office round the corner a million times. And the cab-driver's face said it all when you handed him

135

the big money. Do you really think Tony missed that? You idiot! You're in trouble, Keith.'

'Well, look at the state of me. Revenge is sweet, darling, and I'm not scared of him.'

'He said it was St John who ran you down. He got the number.'

'Yeah? Don't shout at me, George. I say it was him. I don't trust him, OK? Got a drink?'

There was a cupboard in the room which contained some old bottles of strong liquor. I hadn't touched the bottles in a year. I drank wine when I was alone. 'Gin or Scotch?' I hoisted up a quarter-filled bottle of each.

'Scotch.' Keith raised the glass to his scabbed lips, sipped and screwed up his eyes in pain. He waited a moment for the stinging to stop and then spoke. 'If I get to Cheryl, she'll tell me where St John keeps his stuff. We don't need to get it back. We just tell the police it's there and where it came from. Let them handle the rest. We just stand back and take notes.'

I finished my drink and poured myself another. 'Can she take much more pressure? I don't think . . .'

'She can take it, she has to,' he said. 'To get out of there . . .' he added.

'OK, but I think Tony has something else on his mind.'

'Look, my idea is dead simple and nobody gets hurt. What's his?'

'I don't know.'

'He wants St John. That's obvious. You know, you killed my brother, you dirty rat, and all that crap. Yes, well, my money's on St John. He probably thinks the Marquis of Queensberry's a poof.'

'That's another thing. Did you have to go on about his boxing career? I thought we were going to get a quick display of his form, the way you were going.' I was leaning back and sipping my drink. Keith's face was serious. 'Well?' I said.

'Robbie Slater just lost his sight, Georgina. Sandino – you

probably never heard of him – well, he died in a fight with your Tony Levi. Levi retired after that. He was out of control. The man's killed before. He could have killed me. I don't like him on the scene. We have to lose him.'

It didn't sound easy, and I didn't know if I wanted to anyway.

Dexter's secretary led me into the large, elegant high-windowed room on the fifth floor of the bronze glass-mirrored building that was Ghea Records, one of the biggest independent music companies in the world. Its founder and major shareholder, Christian Dexter, was sitting at his desk, clad in jeans and a fashionable oversized sweater, cutting squares of notepaper into spirals with a pair of steel scissors.

Numerous Christmas cards decorated the shelves along the walls and the window-ledge behind him in the office which otherwise qualified as a tasteful tinsel-free zone. When I reached the wide semicircular desk, he stopped snipping and extended a long-fingered hand in the direction of a spartan black leather chair to the right of me. His personal computer sat lifelessly on the desk's black ash surface and there was music playing, something I hadn't heard before. He pressed a button, and it died.

'Let's get right to the point, OK? Keith's tape is of very poor quality. Mick doesn't appear to have a master. I want yours.' He finished speaking and looked down to inspect his hands. His fingers were exceptionally long, even for a tall man. The nails were neat and clipped, like Tony's, clean, unworked. I got the feeling that when he looked up he expected me to have gone, seeing to the matter straight away.

'I can't believe that. Mick has to have it on disk somewhere,' I said.

'Apparently not. So, perhaps you would be good enough to return the copy you have. Carla's copy,' he said, digging under one nail now with one pointed edge of the scissors.

137

His scraped-back blond hair emphasised the Slavic sweep of his cheekbones and square jaw. He was a handsome man but not attractive, to me at any rate. I remembered how he had spoken to Carla, drilled her with his eyes like a magician in a pantomime. It was an act, just as this casual slouch was an act. Every victim had to be treated slightly differently. I wondered how he would react to defeat.

'Might be a little difficult. I'll have to talk to my partner,' I replied.

Dexter placed the scissors carefully on the table and looked up. 'Do what you can, otherwise our legal department will be getting involved.' He was looking straight at me now, his large pale eyes, blue and shiny as starling's eggs, glistened. 'All right?' He was making sure I'd understood.

'Tony Levi . . .'

'Ah yes, Tony Levi. St John tells me you're on to a story about my wife and his unfortunate brother.'

He surprised me. I didn't expect to get that out in the open so soon, but St John hadn't told him the half of it. 'Well, it seems she knew him, and now he's dead,' I said.

'So she knew him, so what?'

'He was murdered.'

'I read the story in the paper. The police said drug dealers. Keith made a foolish attempt to implicate my company, and Keith lost his job, as I recall. No hard feelings on his part.'

'I'm sure there aren't, not now . . . But neither Keith nor the police knew what the killer stole. It seems the dead man was in blackmail business. He took the "Seethru" and "Unreleased" tapes, and some rather compromising pictures of your wife from . . .'

'Look, I know my wife is John St John's mistress, if that's what you're going to say. Cheryl and I married for . . . companionship . . . John St John knows I know. They're not hiding anything from me. We're all still friends.'

'How nice. So you approve of the match?'

'I have no opinion either way. Let's say they're surprisingly suited.'

'So the killer just wanted the report back?' I said.

Dexter's cool look melted a little. 'What report?'

'The Johnny Waits report.'

He got up and walked from behind the desk to the door. He locked it and then disabled his intercom. He sat down again, picked up the scissors and, leaning back, spun the chair from one side to another. 'You've seen this report?'

'No. Tony Levi has seen the printout . . .'

'And made a copy, no doubt?'

'Yes.' I was sure now that Dexter had known nothing about Tommy's haul that St John had done so much to retrieve.

'And what did he make of it?'

'Quite a lot. He says you must have constructed a computer model of the careers of dead stars. You use statistical software to draw conclusions as to whether death is a significant marketing issue in any particular case through correlation and regression analysis. The report said Johnny Waits had to die last November for the sake of a substantial profit hike. Is that true?'

Dexter stretched, and reached into his jeans pocket for a small bunch of keys. Then he leaned over and inserted one dull grey key into a lock at the front of the computer and pressed a button. The screen welcomed him and asked for his password. Shielding his hand from my sight with a wide expanse of back, he tapped in his security code. 'I don't know how St John got that report. It's a misunderstanding,' he said, sitting back down in his chair and swivelling round to face me. 'It was all a game between Johnny and me. You're making too much of it.'

He was smiling now, smugly, and I knew he felt safe. He could say anything; the printed report itself didn't actually prove anything, but I didn't let up.

'But not a game between Tommy Levi and John St John, I trust?'

'What do you mean?' he said, fingering the scissors again.

'I mean, Dexter, that it looks like John St John killed

Tommy Levi to get his little bundle of possessions back. Now that's not a game, is it? Tony Levi certainly doesn't think so, and neither, I imagine, will the police. That little report will interest them. They'll want to have another look at how Johnny Waits died, and Carla Blue.'

Dexter didn't move. The still silence of the office was broken only by distant telephones ringing somewhere else in the building. Loud electronic dance music started up in another room, but it was very quiet in here. Outside, through the smoky glass, clouds were gathering. It looked like snow for Christmas. Dexter rubbed his long fingers against his temples and smoothed a hand back over his scraped-back hair to his ponytail. 'Look, the Spanish police are giving me a hard time about the drugs at the party. I don't need this.'

'Tell me how Carla died.'

'She came down to me. I was sitting by the pool. I told her not to go in because she looked out of it, but she took her clothes off anyway, fooled around with me and then just stepped back. She even swam around awhile. She was conscious when she hit the water. The path report confirms that. Check it, if you like. She started to go under; I went in after her, but I'd drunk my share. She kept going under and then the wave came. It just tumbled over the side and sucked her over. One big easy movement, nothing spectacular, just that . . . and she was gone. I just couldn't save her.' He looked at me for sympathy, but I didn't pity him. I pitied Carla.

'How come the wave didn't take you?'

'It nearly did. I ended up on the side of the pool.'

I smiled. 'You're a lucky man, a real survivor, Dexter. Did you know she'd taken heroin?' I said.

'Not then, no.'

'Do you know why she would have taken it?'

'I don't know. We sniffed coke from time to time, but as far as I know, she wasn't on smack.'

'Your wife is, though, isn't she, Dexter? She must have had some with her. Who gave it to Carla? Did she?'

'I don't know what you're talking about! She might have

given her some – who knows what they got up to – all I know is that Carla's death was an accident. I didn't kill Carla. If someone wanted her dead, then I knew nothing about it.'

Dexter's deep voice had moved up in pitch. The nostrils of his straight smooth unmarked nose flared a little.

I picked my cigarettes out of my bag and lit up, blowing a little smoke across the expanse of his desk towards him. Then I looked over to his computer. 'Don't you think you should check your mail?'

Dexter looked quickly at the machine and then back at me. I gave him an encouraging smile and put my cigarette to my lips. He reached over and pressed some combinations out on the keyboard. The screen filled with text and he looked relieved. 'There's nothing unusual here. What did you want me to find?'

'Nothing. Tell me, what have you got on disk?' I replied.

Dexter turned. His eyes were wet and shinier now. He got up and walked towards a glass drinks-cabinet incorporated into the black modern units that lined the wall. He poured himself a large tumbler of Scotch. Scotch for shock. I refused his offer. 'The stats program, the financial model and the stuff on Johnny. But it's not what you think it is.'

'What is it, then?'

'Look, what do you want? I didn't kill Carla. I didn't plan to kill Carla. We were friends, for God's sake.' His hand gripped his drink.

'So were you and Johnny Waits.'

'I didn't kill her.'

'Did you kill him?'

He didn't answer. It's at times like this when you appreciate how slowly the earth moves on its axis and lumbers elliptically through space around the sun. That afternoon I felt like the tiniest mote clinging to an elephantine partner in the great dance of the planets. I'd got him, or rather, Tony and I had got him. I was sure about Waits, but not about Carla. St John could have been working on his own. Cheryl found out about the program,

141

showed him the printout. He thought about it, decided that Carla should be next. He was at Dexter's party. He had access to Cheryl and her drugs. He could have done it. But Cheryl knows Tommy, Tommy visits her at St John's flat and takes the lot. Threatens to blow the whistle. St John kills him out of jealousy and revenge, and to get his report back. It was possible. Just as it was possible that Dexter had killed Johnny Waits.

'I think I will have a small Scotch, after all,' I said, inhaling a little more smoke and spreading a little more ash on his desk. Dexter poured a shot into a sparkling tumbler and placed it in front of me. 'St John never mentioned the report to you?' I was enjoying the hot pleasant tingle of whisky flowing over my tongue.

'No. Look, it was a game, I told you, between Johnny and me. You're wrong about the rest.'

'How'd he get it?'

'I don't know. Cheryl, I suppose. She must have seen a printout.'

'Did he mention the missing tapes?'

'He mentioned the tapes.'

'Did he mention getting them back?'

'No.'

'Have you got a report on Carla? Has he seen that, too?'

The room was quiet again. The first bars of 'I wish it could be Christmas' billowed along the corridor as someone opened a door. There was a group groan and laughter. The door shut again, and the music faded. I drained my glass and placed it down with an imperceptible knock.

'There are no more reports. I told you it was between Johnny and me, nothing to do with Carla. Carla killed herself, by accident, just like the papers said. I didn't know when she came down to swim what state she was in,' he said.

'St John reckons you had a thing together. Is that true?' I turned to him, trying to control the anger in my voice.

Dexter allowed himself a little smile. 'A thing? We liked each other. We were friends. Everyone needs physical

142

release, so we slept together. She didn't love me and I didn't love her, not in the conventional way. We both wanted some physical sex with someone we could trust. That's all. Does it bother you?'

'No,' I lied. 'Not at all.'

Dexter leaned over and swit.. .d on his pc. He tapped at his keyboard to log in. 'My hard disk is protected, you understand. No one can look in unless they break in, and I can get rid of anything I don't want anyone to see.'

'Are you on the network?' I said.

'Yes, but my information is secure. And if I wanted to wipe any information . . . of a sensitive nature . . . I just press.'

'I wouldn't do that if I were you.'

Dexter's finger remained raised. 'Why, haven't you got a copy of this information you imagine exists?' he said with a sympathetic grin.

'No, it's not that. Ever heard of "Willy's Wild Ride", Christian?' His face told me that he had. 'Good. And before you ask, yes, Willy's in there. I won't tell you what he brought you for Christmas . . . Let's just say it gives me a chance to invite the police in to look over your disk. My advice is, don't try to trash anything.'

Dexter's Slavic face was white now. His fingers hovered over his keyboard. 'What'll happen if I do?'

'You'll be sending half your staff a memo on Johnny Waits, that's what. And if you try and uncouple from the network and delete the files, then it'll just fill your disk up with the stuff. If you dump the disk, the police are going to want to know why. They're going to want to take a look at it.'

He stood up and walked to the window. It was 3 o'clock, and the grey light of the day was disappearing into blackness. He stood reflected by the glass, as I did, wreathed in smoke like someone come to haunt him.

'Do anything to that system, and it'll crash. Then everyone is going to know what you've got to hide,

143

Christian. Everyone is going to know that you did kill Johnny Waits and why, and sooner rather than later. You're going to have problems explaining the smooth distribution of Carla's album in spite of the huge surprise demand and that triple world-wide launch after a tour that was, let's say, only fairly well received in the States. It looks set up, Dexter. It's the sort of profit-making scam that even the City would feel uncomfortable with,' I said, tipping his paper-clips on the table and grinding my cigarette out in their smart metallic container. Then I pushed my chair back and walked over to the locked door. Time to get out of there. I knew Christian Dexter wasn't going to push any buttons. He was cornered. Whatever he did would mean that someone would have to come snooping around his system, see the files, see the program, see the model.

He turned away from the window. 'Why are you doing this?'

My hand gripped the door and I turned back to him. 'If you killed her, I want justice. That's it, OK?'

Dexter smiled as if he saw something in me that he'd seen so many times before. Hypocrisy. 'She talked about you a lot. You were on her mind the night she died, too. She said she'd lost you,' he said. I turned the key in the lock, but he kept on talking. 'I told her if you were as good a friend as she said you were, that would never happen.'

I pulled open the door and walked out. As I stepped out on to the wide pavement of the tree-lined square, I took a deep breath of cold city air and decided to start doing something that I should have done from the beginning: checking up on a few facts, and a few people.

Chapter 12

Detective Inspector Robert Falk had lost weight, but he was still a big man. He sucked on a saffron-coloured chicken-bone and delicately wiped his large freckled fingers on a paper napkin that I had left by his plate. 'How'd you manage it?'

'What?' I said, gathering up the greasy tinfoil containers and emptying them into the pedal-bin.

'Meeting all these, how shall I put it, "dodgy" individuals.'

'I'm a journalist, Robert. *I* am a dodgy individual.'

'Ah, Mrs Powers, life would be easier for you if you were dodgier,' he said, and pressing his steel-framed glasses back up onto his pudgy nose, added wistfully,

'You know, no one calls me Robert, only you.'

'I'm sorry. What would you prefer? What do your friends call you?'

'Bob. But you can call me Robert. I like it. It's so old fashioned and formal.'

I spread the photocopies on the clean kitchen table and stuffed a tin of cold lager into his hand. He peeled open the can and pressed it to his sweet cupid-bow mouth.

'Tony Levi killed a man in '76,' he said, flicking through the cuttings. 'Ah, here it is. I was there, you know.' It was a double-page tabloid spread with a large grimy headline that screamed 'Levi's Killer Blow'. Of course I'd already read it. Robert sat back and relived his memories. 'It was at Wembley, and it was packed. Levi was the local hero. It was

145

a hard fight. Tenth round, Sandino came at him with a fast combination that had Levi backed into a corner. We all thought Levi was in dead trouble because Sandino could punch . . .' He shook his huge head, and took another drink. 'Vicious to the body, he was – and he was really giving it to him. Levi couldn't do a thing but cover up. He took it, and watched Sandino through a high guard and waited, timed it until Sandino put his weight on his right foot. Then he slid along the ropes and turned him. Sandino fell forward, and Levi let go with a straight right counter to the head. End of story. The man went down and didn't come up. Finest welterweight we ever had, Levi. Really clever, very quick and could punch with both hands. Better than Stracey, who was around a bit before him, the WBA champion. The Sandino fight made Levi the number one contender for the world title, but he retired right after it.'

Robert pointed to a large smudgy photograph spread over two pages.

'Sandino – that's him on the floor – died of a brain haemorrhage. There's that story. Well, it was so soon after Robbie Slater. He could have been the champ, but who knows, I mean Sugar Ray Leonard was coming on the scene, and Duran . . .'

I looked over his shoulder at the splayed feet of Sandino, and Tony's raised gloved arms waiting above him. The referee was pressing a desperate arm on Tony's chest to keep him back.

'Robbie's the one he blinded. It doesn't say he died.' Robert pressed his banana fingers down on another cutting and the face of a good-looking black fighter. 'Robbie Slater. Fight before Sandino. Third round, they went on after the bell. Both fighters had been going at each other like pit bulls since the first. They didn't hear the bell after the third. Well, if they did, they weren't prepared to take any notice of it. The long and short is, Slater provoked him and Levi beat him up. That was Levi's weakness – his temper. He couldn't control it. Slater was cut over both eyes and fought for half a round with two detached retinas. Protests followed, Levi got fined. Slater now walks with a white stick.'

'How did Slater provoke him?'

'How do you think? A woman. Levi's sister, as it happens. Slater was stepping out with her and stepping all over her by all accounts.'

'And what happened to the sister?'

'Married one Curtis Cliff.'

'Who's he?'

'Businessman of sorts – lives out in Marbella.' Robert looked up at me leaning over his shoulder. 'Why the sudden interest in boxing, Georgina?'

'Not boxing, Robert. Well, yes, boxing and Tony Levi. The guy's a mystery. He's clever, but he's scary too. Boxers, well . . .'

'You think they're just brawn? Just tough guys who see a way to get up and out of the gutter, get rich through the fight game?'

'Well, I know Tony's bright, but . . .'

Robert looked back at the cuttings, and sighed. 'Boxing is the most beautiful sport in the world. I mean it. It's an art, the art of deception. It's about looking an opponent straight in the eye and making him fear you. It's a game where psychological advantage is as paramount as a devastating left hook or straight right. You don't let the hurt show. You get hit with the guy's best shot and make it look as if it doesn't matter. As Ali once said, you tell him: That the best you got, sucker?'

I thought of my evenings sparring with Tony Levi. How defensive and threatened I'd felt. How hard I'd had to work. He hadn't forgotten the old tricks.

Robert meanwhile had warmed to his subject. 'You listen to a boxer interviewed in the ring after ten rounds and you think he's a dummy. He's got a yobbo accent, he grunts, his vocabulary is poor. He don't know nothing, but he'd like to thank his manager and his mum. He's naked, he's sweating, snot's coming down his nose. His eye's swelling up, and he doesn't care. He's crushed by his manager, his seconds, his mates, his family. They're all dressed up and all over him. He's won, and he's trying to think straight with all the action going on and all his action over. He's triumphant. He's relieved. He's high. He looks disgusting.'

'OK, I understand that, but it's not all that grunting afterwards. I'm not judging it by that. It's the game. It's corrupt, it's violent and crude. Tony Levi doesn't fit in that circus,' I said. 'I don't think.'

Robert blinked his pale bespectacled eyes and ran a hand through his straw-coloured hair. He shook his head. 'You're wrong. Take Mike Tyson. You've heard of him, of course. You read the papers about Mike Tyson. His punching is so devastating the world thinks he can't be human. He's not superman, he's subhuman. He's a brute, and all his unsavoury antics outside the sport are hyped up by the press to reinforce that. He doesn't know how to behave. He beats up his wife. He can make love to twenty women in one night. He's not human. No, he's a gorilla. In the ring, it's his heavy hitting power, his punching, that grab all the attention. Mike Tyson's an animal. Look at him, they say. But they're all wrong. He's a man. No, he's superman. Tyson can punch, sure, but he is the most brilliant exponent of the art of self-defence. The other guys can't hit him to hurt him, you see. That's what destroys them. He blocks their punches, smothers their tactics and sidesteps out of the way. He neutralises their attack and they defend, defend. Then he slips inside his opponent's lead in the blink of an eye and sticks in a couple of lefts. You need split-second timing to do that. You have to be a champion. Ali could do that. He was so sure he could do it that he used to dance around with his hands hanging by his side. Timing and body co-ordination, that's what you need to get away with that. You have to be special. Boxing is a sport that requires tremendous physical fitness, mental agility, courage and skill – and it eats all those qualities up by the shovelful. Oh, and it needs self-discipline. That's how Tyson's going to lose. He's going to beat himself.'

'And that's how Tony Levi lost?' I said, opening up a can of lager for myself.

Robert shrugged his large bulky shoulders. 'All that self-denial, putting your mind and your body through it so you're invulnerable, that's what the training's for, but you can't squeeze everything out. The world's out there – the clubs, the girls, the hangers-on. Levi still had the man in there, inside superman. All covered up, but he was there. He didn't kill Sandino in anger, but he cut Slater up all right. Slater exposed the man, and he suffered for it.'

I sat down and sucked at my drink. Tony Levi, superman. The man with a killer blow. The angry man. 'Is he a face?' I said, and Robert blew out his heavy cheeks.

'Well, he's not a face with the Met and City Company Fraud Unit, Computer Section, that's for sure. All I know about him is what I learned from being on the manor round here. He's got four pubs, three or four shops – maybe more now – a trucking business, a big car and a nice spread in Chigwell – all legitimate, of course. Tommy Levi, his brother, was the one with form. Never liked to work too hard. Spent his time in pubs and clubs chasing the ladies. He did some time for handling, bit of a lad.'

'Drugs?'

'I wouldn't be surprised.'

'What if I said Tony Levi had a strictly illegitimate business?'

'I wouldn't be surprised.' Robert was sifting through some more cuttings. He drew two from the bottom of the pile. 'This is Cheryl LeMat? And this?'

'Yes. The first one's more than ten years old. She must have been eighteen or nineteen. Dexter was her booker at the model agency; that's how they met. He left, founded Ghea and they got married.'

'Oh, I recognise Johnny Waits here. Here he is again, a little thinner . . . Oh, and Carla Blue and her group . . .' He prodded at the pages.

'Band, Robert. No one has a group nowadays; they have a

band. That's Keith, and there's Mick at the back. Keith gets quoted in that one saying how big Big is going to be. Carla also says how big Big is going to be and the only one who doesn't open his mouth to say how big Big is going to be is the one with the brains there, Mick.'

'But you were telling me about Ghea Records. Isn't that what it's all about?'

I nodded and told him about Keith's theory, the report and the virus that was working on Dexter's network. 'The only command it reacts to is "delete". If the virus program receives that message, it substitutes "copy" and the file that Dexter wants deleted is automatically copied to all stations on the network.' Robert rewarded me by saying nothing.

'Well?' I said.

'Well done,' he replied, opening another can of lager with a gentle hiss.

'You'll help me?'

'Of course. What are friends for, Mrs Powers?'

I didn't want to admit that I didn't really know what they were for any more.

Robert Falk made sure I got first call on the story of his team's raid on Ghea Records. The revelation that there was new evidence over Johnny Waits's death made sure my story went front page in the most sensational tabloid fashion. Keith was furious with my return to form. He said it was his story.

I wasn't too bothered about that. I'd wanted Robert Falk to search Ghea's files not just for the stuff on Johnny Waits but on Carla and anyone else Dexter had targeted with his little program. But Robert had bad news for me. There were no other files. There was just the one, the one on Johnny Waits that Tony Levi had described. Dexter had been telling the truth, and it didn't take long for St John to track me down.

'I want to see you. You need to be fucking told,' he said.

'Mind if I bring someone with me?'

'Who? Big Keith, the one with the big theories?'

'No, Tony Levi, actually.'

'That deadshit's brother?'

'Try to be nice, St John. He's got a terrible temper,' I said sweetly.

'Oh boy, I'm filling my pants here,' he said. 'Look, get down to the London Arena tonight. Tell security you got an appointment with me. I got to get things straight with you.'

'Listen, St John, just don't try anything heavy. The police are on the case now, OK?'

'Just fucking get here.'

Strangeways, a misogynist troup of intergalactic troubadours, were playing a pre-Christmas concert at the Docklands venue. They had a big following with the studs and leather boys who liked the fast-fingered fretwork that featured in every other unsophisticated Strangeways lament. There'd be a lot of stuff on sky riders, card games with the devil and odes to mystery mistresses invariably called 'my woman'. Not a jingle of Santa Claus to be had, but none the less appealing. At least, when we got there, the place would be busy backstage and out in front.

Tony had a new car, another BMW, just like the other. He pulled on the handbrake but kept the engine running. 'I'll drop you off here, OK?'

'What do you mean? Aren't you coming?'

'No. Something's come up. Got something else to do tonight.'

'Great.'

'You worried about seeing him alone?'

'Oh no. He's just a little mad with me, but . . . So what? Of course I am, what do you think?' We sat in the car, staring straight ahead, neither of us moving. Then I turned slowly to look at him. 'You're up to something, aren't you?'

'What do you mean?'

'Tony, I want to know what he has to say first, to hear him out and, if needs be, call the police.'

'OK. So what?'

'So. You're going to do something to him, tonight. I know

it. Don't be a fool.'

'You know something,' he said, turning to face me. 'You're a bright girl, but sometimes you really need it spelled out for you. Let that St John spell it out for you. I told you I got something else to do tonight.'

The warm breeze from the car's exhaust whistled up my skirt and I stood alone in the expanse of the car park, watching headlights come winding down through the Isle of Dogs to the vast hangar of the London Arena. Damp icy drops fell on to my face from out of the dark. Snow. Christmas snow. City snow. I could see it touching the ground and melting into greasy blackness. God. I used to run through fields and pick up white crunchy handfuls to stuff in my mouth. My cheeks would burn with the ice in the air and puffs of steamy breath rose up with my laughter. Black birds and stick trees against a white sky, and a snowman in the garden wearing my father's hat, smoking his pipe, gleaming with coal buttons, real coal buttons. I didn't like the snow now. It matted my hair and made my nose drip. It wasn't clean any more.

I walked through the car park to the back of the building. There were another two hours until the concert, and roadies were unloading last-minute equipment from the back of a large lorry. I heard St John's voice first. He was standing just outside the loading bay, bawling out some guy with a clipboard. I walked towards him, and St John waved the man away. He beckoned to me with a stiff gloved paw and stepped back under cover, slipping a hip flask from under his coat. His nose and ears were rosy with cold and his damp sandy hair was speckled with snowflakes.

'Irish. Want some?' he said, unscrewing the top and handing me the flask. It smelled warm and peaty.

'Sure,' I said, taking it and placing the cold metal mouth against mine. There was a loud crash and an electronic wow-wow howl from the stage area.

'Let's get to the point. What you got against Dexter?'

'Everything,' I said.

'You've ruined him, you know that?'

'Well, not quite. That business has got to be worth £400 million.'

'It ain't worth a canned fart when you're in fucking jail.'

'Well, why don't you take the rap, St John?'

His face threw off any fraternal concern it wore for Christian Dexter and concentrated on this new proposition. 'What?'

'First, Carla. Second, Tommy Levi.'

'Fucking what?'

'Come on. You saw the report on Johnny Waits. Cheryl LeMat showed it to you. You must have thought "What a great business proposition, let's try it out on Carla." It was easy, wasn't it? Carla thought she was sniffing coke, you made sure she was sniffing Cheryl's stash of smack. Goodbye, Carla. Hello, big money. Tommy Levi came into view when he spent the night at your place and took the tapes, the photos and the Johnny Waits report. He blackmailed you, you killed him and got the lot back. All neat and safe. What I don't understand is why you tried to kill Keith the other night.'

St John stood silently in the din and the noise with his hair sticking up and his face steaming in the cold air. 'You're crazy,' he said at last. 'I call you here to put you straight on Dexter and you come out with this . . . this *shit*. Fucking *dyke*!' His voice had risen up and out into a roar.

Before I could move, he had the front of my jacket in his fists and had lifted me up and around against the door. As I struggled to pull his hands from my throat, my head connected with something hard and the stage and the lights seem to judder in front of me. I heard men's voices shouting, and St John was hauled backwards. He hung on to me like a dog worrying a bone and I tumbled over him. I rolled away and lifted myself to my knees to run, but as I rose, he grabbed my leg and tugged back. I fell forward, grazing my palms in an effort to save my chin. I kicked his grasping hand away and someone lifted me into the air and over to one side. Then there were two quick cracking smacks. St John skidded back at least six feet on the floor. It took him five full minutes to come round.

Tony Levi's awesome display of boxing skill prevented some of the larger roadies from immediately stepping forward and avenging St John's honour. In any case, the general view was that someone had to take him out for roughing up the lady – that was me – even if she was a dyke.

Nevertheless there was a lot of haranguing over St John's prone body until his eyes opened. Then Tony squatted down and tapped him lightly on the cheek.

'Let's go somewhere quiet and talk, yeah?' he said, and everyone stood back to let St John up. The quietest place was out in the cold night air, in the car park by Tony's new car.

St John's hand rubbed at his puffy jaw. 'Tony Levi. Yeah, I should've known. Great welterweight. Took out Sandino, and that mouthy black git, Slater. I never knew why you retired. You had it. Both hands. Sharp. Could've taken the world title. Why didn't you, instead of coming here and making my life a fucking misery?'

I was beginning to shiver. My head felt bruised, and my hands were raw. I leaned my hip against Tony's dark wet car and watched him. He was enjoying himself. His eyes were twinkling with the lights of the hall, and his lips twitched upward with an unfriendly grin.

St John was unnerved by the cold smiling silence. 'Look. Don't listen to her. She's a dyke. Don't trust her. I didn't kill your brother, I swear to God. He asked me for money, a lot of money, but I didn't kill him. I don't want to know what happened to him. All I want to know is where the photos are. It don't matter about the report now.'

'Well, I only got one. And the lady here swears you got the rest.'

'The fuck she knows.'

'What about Carla? What about Johnny Waits?' I said. My voice was high pitched and accusatory.

St John pulled his lip down. There was a wound gaping where his square stubby teeth had dug in. 'That a cut there?'

Tony looked, and nodded. 'Tell her,' he said.

St John's eyes widened with anger. 'I wanted to tell her, before she came out with all that *crap* . . . Look, Cheryl brought me the printout on Johnny. Sure, I was surprised, who wouldn't be? She was ha'f hysterical about it. I knew all about it. Chris was always pidding about with his computer, making things happen. He showed me the model he'd done on the sales of stars after their deaths. It wasn't anything serious. We had a laugh about it. But they'd made a deal, the two of them, Chris and Johnny.'

'A deal? Is that what he meant by a game between them?' I said.

'I don't know what he said. Johnny Waits had full-blown AIDS, OK? He knew he was going to die. And who the fuck wants to go like that? So they planned it. I knew for sure when I saw the report. But I'd known something was up before that. I guessed that Chris had helped Johnny OD and made sure he died. It wasn't murder, it was an act of fucking mercy. You ever had smack? It's like heaven on earth, it's good news when it hits, I can tell you. I took it twice and let it be. Johnny Waits wanted to go, with dignity, without pain, and filthy stinking rich. What's wrong with that, ferchrissakes?'

'What about his contract?'

'The deal was that his estate got the lot, of course. Ghea had rights to all the stuff it produced with Johnny anyway. Normal business deal.'

'There was no report on Carla, then?' I said.

'No, there was no fucking report on Carla. Who'd want to kill Carla? Chris didn't kill her; he nearly killed himself trying to save her that night. I didn't kill her. Why should I kill her, the biggest damned star I've had in years? Geddoutafit.'

'You killed her because Dexter's computer worked out she'd be a bigger star dead, that's why. You knew "Seethru" was going to be crap. The album would have done nothing if she'd been alive. You gain from her contract, and so does Ghea.'

St John looked as if he were going to lunge for me again.

Tony placed his arm on the roof of the car between us. St John held himself in check and spat a few words my way. 'Crap! Who says? You say. It was right for the market. Spot on. Not right for a couple of hundred poxy clubbers maybe, but millions of kids who wanted to listen to her. She'd crossed over, OK? You little troublemaking shit. Fucking dyke.'

Now I wanted to lunge at him, but Tony diplomatically changed the subject. 'I saw you take out that Keith geezer the other night. He thought it was me. Torched my car. Vindictive bastard, don't you think?'

St John looked away. He started to twitch his left leg back and forth with some emotion. His hand was up at his mouth, chewing at his thumb. 'He screws her. I know he does,' he said, and his eyes filled with water.

Chapter 13

Tony left me in the bar with a large Scotch and water while he went upstairs to check on his dogs. That's what he said he was going to do, anyway. By the time he came back down, I'd bought myself another. The grazes on my hand had stopped stinging, but I felt scruffy. The mud and grease from the concrete floor clung to my damp clothes.

He looked as if he'd done nothing more arduous than deliver a box of chocolates. There wasn't a mark on him, but even so, when he returned, he'd changed into a suit, dark, hand-stitched, with a white shirt and wider than usual deep red tie. It was printed with dark amoeboid shapes and clipped to his shirt with the golden initials, TL, dotted with one little diamond.

'Going out somewhere?' I said.

'I told you I got something to do tonight.'

'Mind taking me home first? Or shall I call one of your cabs?' I said.

'We'll get a cab. Not a nice area, yours, is it?'

He told the driver to wait, and accompanied me to the sixth floor. I unlocked the door and he walked in, switching on the lights and checking the place out. 'Don't it scare you, living in a place like this?' he said, as I shut the door and took off my coat.

'No. People like you scare me when you come in and make out there might be someone in every cupboard. Who are you expecting?' I said, searching in my bag for a cigarette.

'Look, we know, right? Whoever it was killed Tommy and

your pal knows, right? I'm just being careful.'

'Yes, I know, but you don't really expect them to sit in here all hours waiting for me to get home, do you?'

'Just being careful, all right?'

Tony could have left straight away, but he didn't. He stood in the middle of the room as if waiting for something. A big thankyou for saving my life, I suppose. I lit up and took a long drag, looking at him through screwed up eyes.

'You want to get a dog,' he said.

'Why not two?'

'Yeah. Why not?'

'Because . . .' I said. 'Because dogs need routine. I have no routine. They need walkies. I don't take walkies. They need pats on the head. I don't pat heads. They need someone they can rely on. I'm unreliable.'

He didn't reply. Neither of us had thought to sit down. We stood yards apart in my front room, waiting for something to happen. Tony didn't look as if he were leaving. I spoke first.

'You know, I might go out later, too. I think I know where Keith'll be tonight. Might have a little chat. See what he's been up to. What do you think?' Tony didn't say what he thought. He just gave me the dead-eye look. 'Do you believe St John, Tony?' I said, dropping the length of my cigarette into an ashtray and walking past him into the bedroom. 'Oh . . . have a drink. There's some in the cupboard by the phone,' I called, but he was already standing by the bedroom door watching me unlace my boots.

'I got a cab waiting,' he said.

'Sorry, I forgot. You didn't answer me. Do you believe St John?'

'Do you?'

I sighed. 'Do you? *Do* you? Christ! Can't you answer a question? Yes, I believe him, so now what?'

I lifted my skirt a little and began rolling down my lycra tights with great effort. When they were bunched up by my knees, I looked up at him. 'How come you came back, Tony? Back to the rescue.'

No answer. I pushed the tights further down my legs to my ankles. My calves looked very smooth and white against the dark folds of stretched material. I looked down at them for a moment and stared for a long time at the point where my thighs disappeared up my skirt. 'Everyone thinks I'm a dyke, you know that? And it's all that bloody Carla's fault,' I said, dragging off my tights with my heels. 'She kissed me, you know. Biggest shock of my life. Worse than finding the old man with my best friend. Takes the ground from under your feet when you finally discover things aren't what they seem, d'you know what I mean?'

He started to laugh: Tommy's laugh again, a real one. Not a cruel sniff or a cynical grin, a real one. Soon he was laughing so much he had to lean on the doorframe, but he still didn't answer. I kicked my tights off and got up. 'Nice legs,' he said, still laughing, but coughing a little now, 'for a dyke.'

I pulled my jumper out of the waistband of my skirt. 'I'm not a dyke. She was, and because I was her friend, well . . . you know . . . I get lumbered,' I said, pulling the jumper right up over my head, and tugging the neck over my hairline. Then I turned to him, hands on hips wearing nothing but a creamy lace bra, a black stretch mini and a defiant look. 'I'm not a dyke,' I said. He still didn't answer. He just looked. 'You don't believe me?' I said.

He wasn't laughing now because I was walking straight over to him to press my lips on his mouth. As soon as I'd done it, I knew I'd gone too far, and I opened my eyes expecting to see his open too, punishing me. But they were shut tight and he wasn't pushing me away, he was pulling me close. Everything was happening so fast, his hands moving, my hands moving. I was pushing off his jacket and he was tugging at my skirt, our lips fusing together like hot melting fudge. Then it stopped. His hands smoothed down the straps of my bra and he stepped back. He held me stiffly at arm's length and my mind jerked back from a soft dark place to the dim light of my room.

'I got to go. I'm late,' he said.

'What for?'

'Look . . . You don't have to prove nothing. You're OK. I got something to do tonight.'

An icy anger had cleared the heat from my skin and the Scotch from my brain. My hands hurt, and I felt cheated. '*I* know I don't have to prove anything,' I said. 'Do you?' No answer. I stood back and folded my arms. 'All right. Go now. Your cab is waiting.'

'Look, Georgina . . .'

'Out!'

He straightened his jacket and his tie, and left. I listened to his footsteps on the landing and felt the silence in my room. Then I walked to the kitchen, where I made myself a sandwich and poured myself another drink. Might as well stick to Scotch. Christ, what a disaster. And what if he was right? What if that's what I was really doing. Wanting to make love to him to prove what I was to myself. I felt about fifteen: amateurish, gawky and ambivalent.

Time was when all I wanted was to be a boy. Well, if not quite a boy, then not a girl that boys expected to meet, not the sort that couldn't do anything at all, like thread a worm on a hook or bust a conker. It had nothing to do with sexuality. It had to do with identity and pleasing yourself. But that all changed when my breasts grew. Even when they're small, the things are so obvious. Femininity crept up on me from the inside and the outside. I was ripening up for something, but nothing in the real world could convince me of what it was. Boys were so revolting and backward and idiotic. Everyone I knew seemed to have winkled out at least one whose name they wrote in a heart inside their ring binders. It was a serious peer-group problem not fancying any of the boys at sixth form college. Worse still, them not fancying me. It was so isolating. It wasn't so much not being able to join in the busy Darwinian game of selection, it was not feeling the urge to. That was the worrying thing, not having the urge. They fancied Carla, of course. It was easy for her. Carla went out with them crocodile fashion. Carla

Blue. What did I do, to deserve this? I took off the rest of my clothes and looked at them on the bedroom floor. What had I been thinking of, undressing with him there?

'Cheryl?'

'Yes.' Her voice was thick with sleep.

'I'm sorry. Did I wake you?' I said.

'No. Who is it?'

'Georgina Powers.' There was no reply. 'Hello?'

'What can I do for you?'

'Look, I just wanted to call you, to tell you not to worry any more. I'm not after a story. Go to the police. I've got a name. You can talk to him. Tell him what you know.'

'About what?'

'About Tommy. About Johnny Waits. About Carla. Tell him what you know.'

Her voice caught as she answered. 'I can't tell anyone. I don't know anything.'

'You know about John St John.'

She laughed a little, a silly uncommitted cough of amusement. 'Dexter. St John. Pussycats. You don't know what he's like,' she said.

'No. I don't know what you mean.'

'No, I don't suppose you do. Not yet,' she said. Her voice was fading a little. 'He uses people. He used me and Tommy. Now, Tommy's dead. Carla's dead . . . and I'm dead. It's pay-back time. He only leaves the ones alive that he wants to see suffer.' She started to laugh again, again at some private joke. I didn't get it.

Keith rang a quarter of an hour later while I was in the bath.

'I was coming out to look for you at Clam. Thursday night is the Clam, isn't it?' I said.

'I'll be there later. Look, I've just about forgiven you for the Dexter story . . . Cheryl LeMat's going to meet me again. She says the police haven't got a case. Dexter walks. The report is just not enough.'

'Not good for business, though.'

161

'Terrible for business, dearie. The thing's not going to go away, and the weird computer stuff gives everyone the creeps. I heard that some acts are starting to look hard at their contracts. They want to know how they shape up.'

'Understandable.'

'I called Mike Dome, too. The Dudes are sticking with him. He reckons it won't be long before Ghea starts bleeding acts all over the place. Dexter's ruined. He can kiss goodbye to the stock-market placement he had in mind for next year, for sure.'

'You are so well informed, Keith dear.'

'Ah well, I have to be, don't I? It's my job. He could have made himself £300 million at least,' he said, and laughed.

'Did he deserve it, though?' I said.

'You bet he did.'

I wasn't sure, but I didn't tell Keith that. 'Look, I'll see you, but I'm getting cold.'

'Don't tell me you've got no clothes on.'

'All right, I won't,' I said, and replaced the receiver.

The Clam is an unsophisticated cavern that packs a crowd who want to sashay to Latin American sounds and early sixties blues and soul. You would feel warm but not out of place there in black polo-neck jumper, ski pants and a chrome chain. Men dress like Ronnie Kray, and the women like Audrey Hepburn on speed. It's cosy and dark like a party in someone's house. You move through the gloom half expecting to bump into a square of people spliffing up on an LP cover or to stumble into a bedroom laden with pvc, duffle-coats and copulating couples. The ambience, as they say, is cool (as in cat) and intimate (as in contact). There are tables along the walls and dark cubbyholes where people kiss, smoke and talk, and a bright circle where they can dance all night. I used to come here with Carla. We'd wear backless black dresses cut just above the knee, long gloves and sharp little shoes. This was the place where Carla offered me Ecstasy. This was the place to get it, and speed, and coke and smack, girl and boy, I suppose. What did I know? I got my poison from the barman. By eleven thirty, when I walked in, the place was getting crowded. Three-quarters of an hour later, Keith came up behind me and ran his finger down my spine.

'Hi,' I said turning round.

'Well hello, scoop,' he said, and squeezed my buttock.

'Where is she?'

'She should be here soon. I hope she's not shooting up somewhere, or she'll never make it.'

'Great,' I said. I had a feeling she wouldn't show, but I didn't intend to tell Keith about our telephone conversation. Some people moved from their seats, and he ushered me into their vacant little alcove and sat awkwardly stretching his damaged leg under the table. 'St John says he didn't do it.' I accepted one of his cigarettes, and a light.

'Oh yeah? Do you believe that? What about that shark Tony? Does he know about this?'

'Yes.'

'And what does he say?'

'Nothing.'

'OK. Listen, I know St John murdered Tommy Levi because I've talked long and hard to Cheryl LeMat. That Tony Levi knows it, I know he does. Now St John's dangerous, believe me. Scares me shitless every time I meet that girl. I keep expecting him to jump out from somewhere and rip my head off. Anyway, Strangeways are at the London Arena tonight. He's down there for sure, so we should be safe. She says she has proof. I'll get Cheryl to talk to you . . . properly this time, but be nice.'

'Sure.' I didn't tell him about my conversation with St John either.

I put a cigarette to my lips, and Keith saw the scorch on my hand. 'What happened there?' he said, looking concerned.

'I fell,' I said, and looked around.

'You know, you drink too much, Georgie.' He chucked me under the chin.

I didn't have an opportunity to show how nice I could be because Cheryl LeMat never arrived, just as I knew she wouldn't. There was something wrong with her, something wrong about her agreeing to meet us here. She hadn't been in the mood for us tonight. I was sure she'd said more to me than I'd understood. I was just waiting for something to happen.

At first, Keith was annoyed at her. He got up and walked around the club once or twice, peering into corners. He spoke to the barman and the doorman, but the more he drank, the more he seemed to enjoy himself. He offered me a cream-coloured pill. I said No, and eased up on my drinking. The cans were beginning to stack up. I wanted to watch out for trouble tonight, but Keith behaved as if it had never visited his door. He was happy.

'Let's phone her,' I said, but Keith shook his head.

'No guarantee where she'll be. And, anyway, say we phoned St John's place, what if St John answered?'

I stuck an empty can on the pyramid and bit my lip. I couldn't make up my mind. Keith was laughing with a black guy. They gripped each other's thumbs and shook hands. Keith was more relaxed than I was. He knew a lot of people and introduced me to everyone who came up to the table. I nodded and smiled a little uncomfortably at his friends, because Keith never made it clear that we were just friends. He touched me a lot, resting one hand on my shoulder for a time and once sidling under my arm to tweak my breast. I didn't make a fuss. I just kept watching. By two-thirty he said he was ready to go to my place. I said No. He volunteered his place. I said No.

'Tell me something, Georgie. You're not, are you?'

'What?'

'A les.'

'Because I won't go with you? No, I don't think so, but given the mood I'm in, I could be persuaded.'

'It's all right by me. Really. I could fix you up with one . . . s'long as you let me watch.' He thought this was very funny, but when he laughed, it hurt, and he held one side of his chest.

'I'm not, OK? If I was one, I'd have been with Carla, and she might be alive today.'

'Yeah. Well I wouldn't bank on that . . . Oh come on, don't look at me like that, I'm only winding you up. It's all right, really . . . as long as you're not one like Carla.'

'Oh? Why not?'

Keith pulled the tab of another can and took a long swallow. 'She was so cruel . . . You know, cruel . . . A bitch. You're not a bitch, are you? A butch bitch?' He sniggered boozily, amused at this alliterative paradox.

I didn't answer him until he'd taken another long draught of his drink. I felt nervous. Something was happening, but not here. We were in the wrong place, or at least I was. 'You know something, Keith?'

'What's that, my little bivalve?'

'Listen, I'm serious. It's something Tony said. Listen to me. Where is Cheryl LeMat?' I pushed his shoulder hard.

'At home. I dunno. She just didn't come. Don't worry, we'll just have to think of another ruse to nail the bastard.'

'Keith, listen . . . Something's happened to Cheryl LeMat, I'm sure.' He tried to look more sober, and managed to raise one eyebrow over a half-closed eye. 'What's the worst thing that could happen to John St John? Apart from dying, that is.'

'Losing business?'

'No . . . losing Cheryl LeMat. Losing her, don't you see?'

'Yes, I do, I do . . . I do love you, Georgina. Don't worry, they all get what's theirs.' His head fell forward slightly, and his hair covered his pale happy face.

'Do they? He said he wouldn't kill St John. He said it would be worse than that. That's what he'd do. Something worse.' I pushed Keith. 'St John's place in Pimlico. Is that where she stays most of the time?'

'Who?'

'For God's sake, Keith. Cheryl LeMat.' He nodded. 'Do

you know the address?' I pushed him again. 'Come on. Do you know the address?' He nodded. The man was almost asleep. 'I'm going,' I said. 'I'm getting a cab. Let me go.'

It's hard getting a cab at that time in the morning, but by a quarter past three we were on our way. Standing outside in the cold snowy air brought Keith round a little. He began to show an interest in the route. I wanted us to go faster, but when the cab pulled up alongside two police cars outside St John's mews cottage, I knew we hadn't made it. I told the cabbie to wait, got out, and walked up to a uniformed policeman at the door.

'What's going on, officer?' I asked, and he asked who I was.

'I'm . . . We're friends of Cheryl LeMat and John St John. We've been at a nightclub waiting for her. Just thought we'd drop by and see her.'

He looked me up and down as if to take in the look of a person who would drop in on someone at a quarter to four in the morning. He looked into the cab, nodded at Keith, who was struggling to keep his eyes open, and took down our names and addresses. I had to ask before he told us that Cheryl LeMat was dead. I looked at Keith, but his head was already resting on his chest.

It was on the radio, linked to a story about Dexter. Another OD. This time his wife. Body discovered at the home of Carla Blue's manager and long-time friend of the Dexters, John St John. John St John was manager of the late Carla Blue, who also died of a drugs overdose at Christian Dexter's Spanish home. No charges being pressed in the Waits case. Computer software evidence insufficient. Police treating LeMat's death as murder.

The news came chattering through the bed-covers that were covering my head. I looked to the pillow next to me. Mercifully I was alone, and I didn't have a hangover. Pacing, that was the answer. Then I pulled back the covers and looked at the clock. It was gone midday. Pacing, hell. Unconsciousness, more like.

'Robert?'

'I've been calling you all morning, Georgina.'

'Sorry. Unavoidable late night. Have you got the information?'

'Yes.'

'What about the Dexter case?'

'The wife?'

'And that.'

'We can't nail him. Johnny Waits's post-mortem showed a standard drugs overdose. Nothing peculiar at the time. Nothing peculiar now. He had been a user. We can't prove that Dexter did it. There's no evidence, and the computer evidence is far too tenuous.'

'Was Waits HIV positive?'

'Yes.'

'So it could have been a mercy killing. They could have planned it together,' I said.

'He said no such thing to our boys, and he's got an excellent brief.'

'OK. What's the story on his wife. Why murder?'

'She had a history of drugs abuse, Georgina. Heroin.'

'So it was an overdose.'

'No, it was the cut. Scouring powder. Just like Tommy Levi.'

There now. I had it. 'Do you know if anyone's under suspicion?' I said.

'Well, in the light of our little talk the other night, I've suggested to my colleagues that they look back over the Tommy Levi murder and investigate some of the connections you made.'

'Have you managed to get the party list?'

'Oh yes, and I think that will widen the scope of our investigations, as you will no doubt agree.'

I had to make another call, so I tried to hurry Robert along as I jotted down the names of Christian Dexter's guests at his villa the night Carla died. But you can't hurry Robert Falk.

'One more thing, Georgina.'

'Yes, Robert.'

'Don't take any more risks. The police can handle this now. All right?'

'All right. Thanks, Robert. No more risks. You're a pal,' I said, anxious to put down the receiver.

'We should have dinner again soon. I could take you to a fight . . . What do you think?'

'OK, Robert, sounds good, and thanks again.'

I replaced the receiver, and dialled again. Checking. I needed to do some more checking. Oh Christ, I wish I'd done this before.

'Mick. Hi, it's me, Georgina . . . Powers. How's it going? Listen, about this tape that Dexter wants . . . are you sure you haven't got the stuff on disk?'

Mick didn't. He thought Carla had all the copies. In fact, he was sure of it.

Chapter 14

I looked out of the window and down to the car park. It had snowed heavily sometime during the early morning, but dark tyre-marks had ragged it to a threadbare blanket on the grubby ground. I could see a van and a motorbike. Nothing else. He wouldn't be watching me now, if he ever was. He'd be watching him.

I hurried to the telephone and dialled his number. No reply. I dialled the number Tommy had given me, the number of the call phone in the public bar.

Someone picked up the telephone, and battling hard against the noise of the drinking crowd, shouted, 'Who? Who? Tony? Not 'ere, love.'

I rang Keith. His answering machine told me to leave a message. I told him to ring me. I put the telephone down, and it rang back at me almost immediately. There was the beeping noise of a public call-box.

'Hello?' I said, hoping to hurry the caller away with the urgency of my voice.

'George? George, it's me. It's Keith.'

'Are you all right?'

'Yes, I feel like death, of course.'

'Haven't you been home?'

'Yes and no. I didn't make it last night.'

'Didn't the cab take you home? Where are you?'

'At a station. Did you hear the news? I saw it in the paper. They're saying it's murder, Georgie. They say she was poisoned. Bad trip.' I said I knew. 'Well? Who is it,

Georgie? St John or your friend Tony Levi?'

My heart was beating hard now. No risks, that's what Robert said. 'I don't understand.'

'To get at him. At St John. It had to be. And now he's waiting for me with those monster dogs.'

'He's at your place?'

'Well, not exactly outside the door, but I saw him just in time. I told the cab to keep moving, and went to a mate's place. What's he want me for, George?'

I had to think fast. No point in spelling it out yet. 'His car? You burnt his car, and he liked that car, Keith.'

He was trying to put more money into the slot. 'You think he did it? St John wouldn't kill her, would he? It's got to be the other fellow.'

'It's possible. If you're scared, call the police.'

But the buzz on the line told me he'd gone. I replaced the receiver, and looked around as if someone was behind me. But no one was there.

He was at my flat a quarter of an hour later. He looked harassed, and the cold clung around his frozen body as he limped in at the front door.

'What's happening?' I said, offering him a drink.

He slumped back on the sofa, resting his leg on the coffee table. 'Where's your friend?' he said, tapping his pockets for a cigarette packet.

I picked mine off the table and hoped my hand wouldn't shake. 'Tony Levi? I don't know.' I wondered if Keith had been hanging about, watching the block. He looked bluish-white and cold, frowning as he dragged the gin bottle over to his glass.

'I haven't been able to get back to my place. I need to get back. Look at these clothes! I'm fucking freezing. No Scotch?'

'All gone.'

'Anything to go with this?'

'No, I'm sorry.'

'It's OK. I'll drink it straight.' He filled half a tumbler,

170

drank it down, and shuddered. Then he looked up with watery pink eyes and asked if I could switch on the gas fire. 'Can you make me something hot? Some food, some coffee? I haven't slept, and I feel like shit.'

I nodded.

'OK. Where've you been, Keith?' I said, coming out of the kitchen some minutes later with toast and a steaming mug of coffee. He looked at the plate with disappointment. 'I'm sorry, I never have a lot in.' I placed the plate and mug on the table in front of him.

He sucked on a cigarette, and cupped his blotched fingers round it. 'Police took me in. They'd had St John in all night.'

'They let you go?'

'They were asking questions about last night. They'll be wanting to talk to you next. I said I was with you all evening. We were waiting for her. She was going to talk to us about a trendy nightclub story we were working on. I didn't want to expand. Why? You sound surprised,' he said, putting down his cigarette and picking up a slice of buttered toast.

'I thought they'd keep you in for your own safety. They do that, don't they? You did tell them about Tony, didn't you?' I said, thinking quickly. He didn't reply. 'Keith?'

'No, I didn't.'

'Keith . . . why would they think we had anything to do with Cheryl LeMat's death?'

'Christ, I don't know, do I? All I know is that East End wide boy is following me with his dogs.' He was on his feet now and limping agitatedly around the room. He looked out of the window and then turned towards me. 'I told St John it was Levi who killed Cheryl.'

I tried to look shocked. 'But we don't know that! If St John killed Tommy, he'll kill Tony for that. He won't think twice. Why didn't you tell the police? We have to stop them.' I thought my acting was holding together at least as well as his. All the lies, Keith. All the lies.

'I wanted him off my back,' he said. 'I hope the fuckers kill each other, the pair of murdering bastards. They deserve each other, always squeezing the little guys. Well, let them squeeze each other now.'

'But why Tony? What's your beef with Tony? What if he didn't kill her, didn't kill anyone?'

He didn't answer, but sat down again on the sofa and drank a little of his coffee. I sat down opposite and watched him. He was so convincing, so clear about what he was doing, and how right he was. This big spoiled boy with his freckles and his floppy hair was confident in his cruelty, unalarmed at pulling wings off butterflies, trapping frogs in plastic bags. No conscience. Carla was like that. I remembered sitting watching Carla read her verse from the pink and black book: 'Into many a green valley drifts the appalling snow; Time breaks the threaded dances and the diver's brilliant bow.' The piece had worried me, but Carla had liked the rhythm of the words and the sound of her voice saying them, that's all. Where do they get that innocent unfeeling confidence? 'It's over now, Keith. We can't do any more,' I said.

He smiled to himself, and stretched out his damaged leg. 'You're right. They paid for killing Waits and Carla. Dexter with his business and St John with his girl.'

'They paid for Tommy Levi, too, didn't they?'

'What? Oh yes, they did. Big shots. We can do a good story on this . . .' He looked over at me and raised an admonishing eyebrow. 'Together, now.'

I laughed to keep in with his mood, and then said, 'When did Cheryl die? Did the police say?'

''Bout eleven, before St John got to her. That's what he says anyway, and I believe that. The cut was the same that killed Tommy Levi. I think Tony thought about that, and returned the compliment.' Keith picked his half-finished cigarette from the ashtray and lit up again.

I thought about my call to Cheryl last night after Tony had left. It wasn't long after we had spoken that Keith had called. I hadn't called him. Now I understood. You don't know what he's like, she had said, and she had meant Keith. Maybe he was there all the time, watching her talk, waiting to give her another shot, the killer blow.

'So what did you tell the police?'

'I said I was at the club. I was with you. Well, I was, wasn't I?'

I didn't answer that. I just looked away at the window, and back at him. The snow had started falling, and the twilight was blotting out the day. I didn't want him here. I couldn't keep the act going much longer. 'Look, you can't stay. He's bound to think you're here. You have to go. I'm frightened of him, Keith.'

He smoked his cigarette, and then stood up. 'You're right. I've got a mate who'll put me up. Levi won't know the place.'

'Keith, tell the police . . .'

He patted his pockets to check that he had his cigarettes, and then picked them up off the table. He smiled at me. 'Hey . . . What are you doing for Christmas? What say we get away . . . get some sun? We're a good team, you know.'

I tried to give him the sort of look that I always had. 'Keep trying, Keith,' I said and he laughed and left.

When he'd gone, I rang Robert Falk. 'Right, I'll tell the inspector in charge of the investigation. You haven't seen Levi?' he said.

'No.' I ran my fingers through my hair, and inhaled. The air was stale with the smell of cigarettes and booze. I needed a shower. Then I'd open some windows in here, let in the cold, damp snowy air.

I didn't hear the click in the lock as I sat on my rumpled bed, rubbing the moisture from my hair. The first I heard of them was loud panting and a growl like the labouring of demonic pistons in my ear. The door. I hadn't chained the door. I stopped drying my hair and gently drew the damp towel back. They were close enough to press their dark glistening noses against my collarbone. They had only to lift their heads, and their leathery lipped jaws would clamp round my throat. Their hot breath snuffling through glistening yellow teeth smelled of primeval caves, and I sat still, holding on against a dreadful falling feeling of fear.

'Where is he?'

'Get them away from me, Tony . . . Please!'

'Where?'

I hadn't looked at him yet. One of the dogs slapped its iron jaws together with a hard wet clap, and I winced. 'Please. Please, Tony, please!'

'Where is he?'

'I don't know.'

'You're lying.'

'He's been here, and he left. He's going to a friend's. I don't know where. Look, he knows you're after him, he saw you, but he doesn't know that I called the police. Leave it now, Tony. It's over.'

The dogs were growling now, a noise like distant buzz-saws emanating from their throats. I squeezed my eyes tight until he said the word 'Out'. The two dogs lowered their massive heads and backed away into the front room. I tucked in the loose end of my bath towel around my chest and stared at him. His suit was crumpled, his tie was loose, and there was a shadow of stubble on his face.

'When did he leave here?'

'He left about an hour ago,' I said, but there was hardly time to feel relieved.

Tony moved forward and jerked me violently up off the bed, his hard fingers grasping my flesh. 'Where is he?'

The pinching pain made me snap back at him. 'Look, leave me alone! What's your beef with me? You're hurting me, Tony. You're hurting me.'

His eyes were red-rimmed, but more alive than I'd ever seen them. They terrified me. His tough hands gripped my shoulders harder and harder until my skin began to bleed under his nails as his fingers dug down to my bones. I was rigid with pain. He pinned my arms to my side and bent me backwards, forcing my back to arch until there was no way but down. My voice was trapped somewhere in my chest, and I began to choke.

'Where is he? You helped him. Where is he?'

I couldn't see his face now, only his lips and his canine teeth, so close to me that panic made me struggle to lift my numb hands against him. It was useless. He just hauled me over and slammed me down on the bed. My head hit the headboard hard and rolled forward, but he grabbed me again, pulling and shaking me, his legs astride my waist, his arms forcing my body up and down, pumping the breath out of me, until I could manage but one screaming shout of agony. Then he stopped, letting me drop on to the soft pillows. My eyes opened to see him raise his fist. I could see its shattered knuckle and golden rings shining in the light as it came down. I blinked, and the first thing I saw when I opened my eyes again was the pain and frustration in his face as his hand slammed into the wall. Then he was gone, and I rolled naked off the bed, and my knees crashed on to the floor.

I cried for a long time until he came back. He found my dressing-gown lying behind a chair and wrapped it round my stinging, aching body. Then he sat down beside me on the floor, leaning his back against my bed.

'I'm sorry,' he said. 'I'm sorry.'

I sniffed, and wiped my eyes with my hands.

'I'm sorry,' he said.

'You bastard!' I said, and my hand shot out at his face. My palm stung with the slap, but he didn't move. 'Sorry isn't good enough, Tony. I'm not hiding him anywhere. He's out there somewhere. Why should I protect him?' My voice choked more with anger now than pain.

'I'm sorry. I couldn't see . . .'

'Couldn't see me? What am I? Nothing? Just something else to step on? Just something in your way?'

'No.'

My hand struck his face again, and again he didn't move. He hardly looked at me. 'I'm sorry. I couldn't see . . .'

'Save it, Tony.'

He sat leaning against the bed, his face white, his mouth a tight line. 'I suppose I wanted to hurt someone. Yeah, I did. I needed to hurt someone. But I wanted it to be him, not you. I'm sorry,' he said at last.

I pushed my arm down on the floor to get up, but the ache that wrenched my elbow was too much to bear. So I shifted painfully to sit on both buttocks and leaned back next to Tony against my bed.

He put his bloodied hand up to his face for a moment, dragged it down his cheek and wearily away from his face. 'I just lost it . . . I'm sorry.'

'Get me a cigarette, will you . . . and an ashtray? My bag's in the front room somewhere,' I said, shifting my back again to stop some ache somewhere.

He fetched them, and sat down on my bed. I placed a cigarette between my lips, and he leaned over and lit it for me. His hand was very grazed and swollen.

'You didn't get there in time, did you?' I said, puffing the smoke away from him.

'No.'

I carried on smoking, waiting for him.

'He must have already been and gone. I rang the doorbell. No answer. I waited. St John arrived late, and that was it. She'd been in there all the time. The bastard keeps winning.'

'Would you have got there if you hadn't come back for me?'

He shook his head. I looked over at him. He leant an elbow on his knee and rubbed at his closed eyes with his undamaged hand.

'Would you?' I said.

'I should have gone straight away. I went back to my place and got the dogs. I just wasted time. I should have gone straight to St John's place and waited outside. She might be alive now if I'd done that.'

'You've known a long time, haven't you?' I said, leaning painfully forward and flicking ash into the ashtray.

He looked across at me. 'He told St John that you killed her, because you think St John killed Tommy. Keith wants St John to kill you, to protect himself and to finish the job he started with Carla. It wasn't how his plan was supposed to go, but Keith is working by the seat of his pants now.'

I stubbed my half-smoked cigarette out and rose uncomfortably, pulling the dressing-gown down properly round me to cover my body while my bath towel fell to the floor. I limped over to the dressing-table, sat down, and dragged my fingers through my damp hair.

'He won't go back to his place. I told the police I saw him around midnight, not when he said. They'll find the stuff in his flat. Keith's finished.'

Tony sat on the bed, watching me – his eyes glazed with defeat. The records showed that he had never lost a fight. Maybe, I thought, but his victories had been bitter ones.

'He hasn't won,' I said.

'He's alive. All the people he wanted to finish are dead. Finished, or dead. That's what he set out to do. That sounds like winning to me.'

'He hasn't got away with it. That's the important thing. Anyway, you don't think you could have killed him, do you?' I said.

'Yeah.'

'How come?'

'I've done it before.'

'It's not the same, is it? What are you thinking about? Sandino? You didn't intend to kill him, did you? It was an accident. You didn't want to kill him, did you?'

'No, but I did.'

'OK. What about Slater? He was the one you tried to kill, really wanted to kill, wasn't he?' There was no reply. 'Wasn't he?' I said.

Tony didn't look at me. He just nodded his head and said, 'Yeah.'

I sat down on a stool in front of the dressing-table and pulled a wide-toothed comb through my hair. I could see Tony in the mirror staring at my sore back now. There were red weals on my arms and chest. He could probably see others. 'But you didn't, did you?' I said to his reflection.

'What's the difference?'

'Well . . . you wanted to, and you could have done, but you didn't. That's a big difference.'

He got up and stood behind me, touching my shoulders with his hands. His hands were warm and soft now. His rings twinkled on his fingers.

'Don't,' I said, and his hands dropped by his side.

He stood right behind me. I couldn't see his face, just his white-shirted waist and dark trousers.

'What are you going to do?' I said, putting the comb down on the table.

'I dunno.' He turned away and walked towards the door. 'I owe Tommy something.'

'Look, it came out right. Keith didn't win. Keith lost. He's going to go to jail. He's finished.'

'Can I make a coffee?' he said.

I nodded, and by the time he'd brought two cups back, I'd dressed. We went into the front room, where the dogs were by the door, feigning sleep. He sat in his chair, and I sat on the sofa, curling my feet under me. 'Are you going to tell me now?' I said.

He looked up over the steaming cup in his hand, and shrugged. 'I checked with Tommy's mates, that's all. Put some faces to work and came up with Tommy's club scene. He knew Cheryl all right, but through Keith – David he calls himself when he's about. He's the candy man. He supplies. Got stuff off Tommy, supplied her. Then he set St John up. He got all the tapes, the report and the photos from St John's place and gave the lot to Tommy. Tommy thought he was on to a good thing, blackmailing St John. But Keith set St John up, and Dexter. He killed Tommy to start the ball rolling. To make Cheryl think St John had murdered him. The fact that you knew about the pirate tapes meant he could run the story and link Dexter or St John to Tommy. Tommy was nothing to him. St John never took the report, or the photos, or the tapes, or the junk . . . because he didn't kill Tommy. Why'd St John want the junk? To give it to his princess? You must be joking. No, Keith had it. That was a mistake. Keith couldn't leave that heroin behind, could he? That bothered me. He made a mistake. He was too greedy. Wanted to sell it twice. He killed my brother. Probably killed your mate Carla, too. But I don't know why.'

He'd checked. As I should have done right from the start.

'Jealousy. Revenge. He wanted to be a star. He'd come so close, and they – Dexter, St John, Carla, that is – took it away from him. So he ruined them all. He hated Carla, so he killed her. He wanted the others to pay in different ways. Dexter with what he loved, his business and Waits's disgrace, St John with what he loved most, Cheryl. He punished them all, because they stopped him being Mr Big,' I said.

'When did you tumble him?'

'Well . . . if I'd done my job, I'd have done the basic stuff first, but I didn't. I've sort of forgotten what my job is, really. Checking, asking questions. Having a nose for a bit of nonsense, something not quite right. If it wasn't for Keith, I wouldn't have bothered at all. He wanted to keep me going with the whole charade, using me all the time. He made me suspicious about Dexter and Carla, about her death. The story, the report. He fed me with ideas. That was his mistake, too. Your story and his about the car was different, wasn't it? Then there was the business about the tape. I couldn't understand why Keith's tape was so poor. Dexter said Mick didn't have one. That set me thinking. It started me thinking, what if mine was the only copy? Keith would have had to have got it from the counterfeits in Tommy's stash. I checked with Mick. He didn't have one, said Carla had the only one. Then I asked my policeman friend to give me a list of the people at the party.'

'He was there?'

'Yes. Cheryl was there, so he was there. St John was right, he was screwing her. He supplied her with drugs and got his asking price. She had panicked about the report, and he made her think St John had killed Tommy because of it, not because she was sleeping with Tommy, because she wasn't. She knew in the end he was using her. She was afraid of him. He killed Carla. He gave Carla the heroin instead of cocaine. She wasn't experienced enough to know the difference. He hated Carla. Not because he thought he had talent, but he didn't think she had either and couldn't see why she had to be the star.'

'The report was a gift, then.'

'Yes, you can see how it happened, can't you? Cheryl all hysterical because she's stumbled on something which implicates Dexter in a murder. She shows it to St John. St John keeps it under his hat. Keith sees it during one of his jaunts at St John's flat, and sees his chance . . . Poor Tommy was just a prop in all of this, and so was I. You were the only problem.'

I gathered up the cups and took them into the kitchen, where I stood by the sink gazing past the tower blocks at the grey, snowy skies resting over the City. I heard Tony's voice behind me.

'You all right?'

'Yes, I'm all right, Tony. I was just thinking how sick I am of this view. You know, snow can make a brick and slate hovel with dustbins out front look picturesque, but a tower block? No way. Look at it out there and me up here like a canary in a crow's nest. You know, it's sad, but I never really got the hang of this city. No, I don't think I ever did.'

'What are you going to do?'

I looked out of the window and thought about it. It was all over, finished. 'You know, my parents want me home for Christmas. I think I'll go, and maybe I won't come back this time.'

He stood beside me, and touched my arm. 'I'm really sorry . . . what I did before.'

'And last night,' I said, turning to him. 'Are you sorry about that?'

'Yeah, I'm real sorry about that,' he said, and we laughed.

It was hard, but we laughed all the same.

'I wonder if St John'll believe him?' I said. Tony said nothing. 'What'll it be then, drawn BMWs at dawn?' I was still looking out through the cold dirty windowpane.

'I don't think so. Maybe I can talk to him,' Tony replied, standing really close now, his hands turning me round.

Chapter 15

The ducks on Victoria Park pond were sliding on their backsides on the ice to the groups of people throwing bread for them. There was no wind, just cold crisp air all around keeping the snow compact on the ground and patches of ice on the pavements. I was drinking hot tea from a white plastic cup when I saw Tony coming through the gate. He wore a thick sheepskin coat over dark trousers, and walked with his head down and his hands thrust into his pocket. I threw the cup into a wire basket stuffed with frozen rubbish.

'Fancy a walk?' he said, keeping his hands in his pockets.

'Why not?' We turned together to walk along the path past the deer who stood still under the trees, blowing white clouds of breath into the air.

'When are you going?'

'Saturday. I'll be home for Christmas Eve on Sunday. I suppose you'll be pretty busy?' He shrugged. 'Well, won't you?' I said, stopping and poking him in the chest.

'Yeah, we'll be busy all right,' he said, pulling a buff-coloured envelope out of his pocket and handing it to me.

'£12,800, your cut.'

I stared at the envelope and then up at him, and smiled. 'Thanks,' I said, tucking it into my shoulder-bag. 'Thanks very much.'

'How d'you feel?' he said.

'Oh, pretty good, considering. Keith got arrested. St John came apart at her funeral. Dexter had to hold him up. He had two black eyes . . . St John, I mean.'

'Well, he took some convincing . . .'

I smiled. 'And I've had more work to do than I've had in the past two years.'

'That's good, isn't it?' he said.

'I suppose so.'

Tony put his hand on my arm and started us walking again. 'Listen, about your flat . . . are you going back to it after Christmas?'

'Just to pick up my things,' I said. 'Why?'

'Well, someone I know'll give you three grand key money for it. Don't want to lose a place like that.'

'Des.Res.Bow? Oh no, you're so right, what with the view and everything . . .' Tony looked exasperated, and I tucked my arm under his and stepped forward. 'Look, the tape's one thing, but no deal on the flat. It ought to go to someone who's waiting, on the list,' I said.

'You leaving the lot? Leaving it like it is?' he said.

'Oh, it's hardly luxury, and it was never mine. I didn't buy a thing for that place. Warren did. Thought I'd like it. Let someone else have it.'

We walked on. Tony's face was glum. 'That's it, then?' he said.

'That's it.'

'Where are you going?' he said, stopping again to rub his soft leather gloves together and look away across the white park.

'California, maybe.'

'What's there?'

'Sunshine. Some friends. My ex-husband. No trouble, I hope.'

Tony looked down at his watch. 'They've been open half an hour. Fancy a drink?'

'Then what?'

Tony's eyes were blank. 'We could go to my place in Chigwell. Perhaps we could exchange gifts,' he said, and I laughed. He laughed, too. Tommy's laugh.

Then I looked up at the cold grey sky and put my gloved hand to my mouth. Goodbye, Carla, I thought. Here's a goodbye kiss.